DRUMSHEE
Chronicles

A LIFE FOR A LIFE

Cora Harrison

MENTOR
BOOKS

This Edition first published 2005 by

MENTOR BOOKS
43 Furze Road,
Sandyford Industrial Estate,
Dublin 18.
Tel. +353 1 295 2112   Fax. +353 1 295 2114
e-mail: all@mentorbooks.ie
www.mentorbooks.ie

ISBN: 1-84210-292-3
·A catalogue record for this book
is available from the British Library

Cover design/illustration: Alphabet Soup/Allied Artists, UK
Edited by Claire Haugh
Design and Layout by Mentor Books

Printed in Ireland by ColourBooks Ltd.

Contents

FOR MY GRANDSON
SHANE MASON

The Real Drumshee

Often my readers ask me whether Drumshee is a real place and the answer to that is: yes, it is a real place, a small farm in County Clare in the west of Ireland, but I made up the name 'Drumshee'.

I have not been able to find out much history connected with 'Drumshee' but it is almost certain that the farm was continually occupied since the Iron Age. There is a big Iron Age fort on the top of the hill with a magnificent ditch and the remains of a high wall around it. The people would have lived in small stone houses within the walls.

At some stage, probably in medieval times, there must have been a castle built inside the enclosing wall of the fort as there are many huge, beautifully cut stones on the farm. These include some battlements from the top of the castle, possibly some of the spiral staircase and also a stone with a latch hole cut at the side of it. These stones date to the late medieval time. There is also a tiny casement window – with almost no glass left in it, except tiny pieces of greenish, bubbly glass in the corners of the metal strips that form the diamond pattern on the window. This is undoubtedly from the castle, also.

When the castle was demolished, a cottage with thick stone walls and a thatched roof (later a stone roof) was built outside the walls of the fort – and that is where I live today, on a farm of twenty acres.

If you want to know more about Drumshee, or about me, log on to www.coraharrison.com.

Chapter 1

The call for help came on a wet night in May.

17th May 1318. Fidelma had just written on her vellum book of poems. She paused for a moment, stroked the silky springy tip of the feather pen against her cheek, and looked out of the castle window. The old ash tree outside the walls of the castle enclosure was bending and swaying in the wind, and billowy clouds of wet mist swept across the valley of the River Fergus. I am fifteen years old, she thought, and I have never managed to capture all this beauty in a poem.

And it was at that moment that a loud hammering came on the oak door of the castle.

'O'Malachy!' came the shout. 'Open up, O'Malachy! Conor O'Dea needs your help.'

Fidelma's father, The O'Malachy, jumped to his feet.

'Why doesn't someone open up? he said. 'When Conor O'Dea calls, the O'Malachy clan answer immediately.'

Sixteen-year-old Shane was ahead of him, however, and was through the door before his father had dragged on his leather jerkin. Fidelma followed him, but stayed standing at the top of the stairs. With three bounds, taking six steps at a time, Shane was in the Great Hall and had opened the door before Conall emerged from the kitchen.

The man on the doorstep was dripping wet and hoarse from shouting. He looked past Shane to O'Malachy who was stumping heavily down the stairs.

'Can you bring some men, O'Malachy?' he croaked. 'We're lost unless we can get help. De Clare and his Norman troops are camped outside Ruan. They're only ten miles from us. Conor O'Dea has sent messages to Loglen Og O'Hehir of Magowna, and to Felim O'Connor of Fisherstreet, but you are nearer. How many men can you bring?'

'I've thirty men-at-arms standing by,' said Donald O'Malachy steadily.

'Thirty-one,' said Shane.

Fidelma shivered. Something told her that this night would bring great danger. Perhaps her beloved brother would be killed this night.

'Thirty,' said O'Malachy. 'You stay here, boy, with your mother and your sister. This will be a bad fight.

You know how de Clare, cursed Norman that he is, killed your mother's grandfather and now occupies his castle at Bunratty.'

'We need every man-at-arms that we can get,' said the messenger. The words jerked out of him through the knotted cords in his throat.

'I'm going,' said Shane quietly. He cast a quick glance up the stairs. His mother had come out of the solar, and was looking down. Her hand was at her throat.

'I have to go,' said Shane more loudly. 'For the honour of the O'Malachys, I have to go.'

Donald O'Malachy nodded. He cast a quick glance up at his wife, but then turned his eyes away. The honour of the O'Malachys was important to him, too.

'I'll sound the alarm,' he said. 'Conall, give this man something to drink and a fresh horse.'

'I'll sound the alarm,' said Shane. In a moment he was outside, leaving the door wide open behind him. The south wind blew strongly through the open doorway and lifted the tapestries and painted leather hangings from the walls. Maur O'Malachy turned and went back into the small cosy solar. She would weep there, Fidelma surmised, but she would not stop Shane. He was a young man, now, and his mother would know that the honour of the O'Malachys would be all-important to him. Fidelma did not follow her. Her mother would not welcome her company at this moment. Holding up her long dress in one hand Fidelma ran down the stairs, crossed the Hall and stood at the doorway.

The great bell at the gate began to toll. The wind would pick up its solemn message and all of the able-bodied tenants and their sons would snatch their weapons from the walls of their cottages and soon they would be at the castle.

The torches flared in the courtyard now and the tall iron gates were flung open. Once, long, long ago, this courtyard had been the inner enclosure of the fort of the ancient people of Drumshee. Almost a hundred years ago, Malachy, the great-grandfather of Shane and Fidelma, had built his castle, four storeys high, within its walls. Beside the walls he had built stables for his horses and Fidelma could see Shane going over towards them now.

'Shane,' she called out. 'I'll saddle your horse. You get yourself ready. Put on the padded leather jerkin. That will keep you safe.'

He nodded. The pale cream of his skin was flushed with excitement. His blue eyes sparkled. He crossed back over the courtyard in three strides of his long legs.

'See mother before you go,' she murmured as he passed her.

He nodded again. For a moment the burning blue

of his eyes seemed to cloud over, but then the shadow passed. He was a man now and he had to fight when his neighbours and friends called for assistance. That was the way that the clans worked; Fidelma knew that. When he spoke his voice was light-hearted and joking.

'It's raining hard. You'd better put on your cloak and cover up that fancy hair style,' he said. He touched her head where the heavy rich-brown hair was braided and looped under the net of fine gold, and then he was gone, bounding up the stairs.

Fidelma took down her fur-lined cloak of brushed wool, threw the hood over her head and went out into the rain. Con O'Donoghue, his son, and three men-at-arms were coming in through the gate, the light from the torches flashing on their short swords. There was a sound of hoofs on the avenue. That would be the O'Neilans, she guessed. All the clans were gathering. They would go forth under the leadership of The O'Malachy of Drumshee. Perhaps they would all be back by this time tomorrow, she told herself, but somehow she could not banish the feeling of blank horror in her mind.

When she opened the stable door, Shane's horse was already stamping and blowing heavily. He sensed the excitement.

'Easy, boy, easy,' she murmured slipping the bridle

over his head and then fitting the flat leather saddle across the broad muscular back. Shane had got this magnificent black stallion for his sixteenth birthday and it was the best horse in the stables.

'Take care with him, now,' warned Brian the stableman who was busy saddling her father's horse. 'He'll burst out as soon as you open his stall door. He's a highly-strung fellow; he knows there's something amiss.'

'I'll be all right,' said Fidelma confidently. She blew into the horse's nostrils and then placed her hand across them and whispered into his small, elegantly-pointed ear. 'You'll keep him safe, Bel, won't you?'

Then she opened the stall door and led him across the yard to the front door of the castle. Shane was already there; so was her father, but there was no sign of her mother.

'Fly my hawk for me, Fidelma, if we're not back by tomorrow,' Shane said as he swung himself on to the horse.

'God bless us and save us, don't be saying that,' said Brian, his right hand automatically flicking the sign of the cross over his face and chest. O'Malachy said nothing, however; his face was grave. There was danger in this expedition; Fidelma knew that by the look on her father's face. Fighting the Normans was a different matter to fighting unfriendly clans. The Normans were better armed, and better protected with their suits of chain mail, than the native Irish. Edward Bruce, the brother of the Scottish king, Robert Bruce, had come over to help the Irish fight these Normans, but all over the country the Normans had won the battles and now Edward Bruce was dead – killed at Dundalk. She looked around her. The courtyard was filling up with the tenants who farmed her father's four thousand acres. And every one of those faces bore the same grim look. This would be a fight to the death for many of them.

'In the name of God, let us go,' said O'Malachy. He raised his right hand, holding his sword aloft and the candlelight streaming out of the Great Hall sparkled on its blade and for a moment the drops of rainwater turned the iron into a brilliant rainbow.

'O'Malachy, *abú*,' shouted his men.

'O'Malachy, *abú*,' shouted Shane, his voice still high and sweet-toned.

And then they were gone through the gate: first O'Malachy himself, then the O'Donoghues, the Carneys, the O'Neilans, the O'Hegartys, the McMahons, the Queallys – thirty men-at-arms and then, last of all, Shane. They all went through the gate without a backward glance, except the last of the riders. At the great gates, Shane reined in his horse and turned and looked back as if he were taking his last look at the tall grey stone castle. He lifted one hand, whether in salute to his sister, or to his home, Fidelma did not know, but then he, too, was gone.

 # Chapter 2

O'Malachy and his men made slow progress through the wet fields and muddy lanes. It was well after midnight by the time that they arrived at The O'Dea's castle, but the flaring torches and the noise of hammering showed that no one was sleeping. The smiths would be working all night to make as many new iron-tipped arrows as they could, thought O'Malachy. He sighed to himself. The Irish short-bow would not be much use against the longbows of the Normans.

'Thank God for good neighbours,' came a voice when they pulled up at the gatehouse. The words were quietly spoken, but the relief was obvious on the face of the young man who had come down the steps from the castle.

'This is a fight for all of us, O'Dea,' grunted O'Malachy swinging a foot over his horse's back. 'Good lad,' he added as Shane nimbly leaped from his own horse and, holding the bridle in one hand, helped his father down with the other hand.

'You here, too, Shane,' said Conor O'Dea. 'How's the hawk?'

'Good,' said Shane briefly. This was not a moment for talk of hawks; he knew that. Conor O'Dea's face was drawn and anxious.

'Any news of O'Hehir and O'Conor?' asked O'Malachy.

'I don't expect them before noon, but de Clare and the Norman knights will be at our doors before then. They'll surround the castle and trap us inside. O'Hehir and O'Conor won't be able to do much for us then.'

'How long can you last inside the castle walls?' asked O'Malachy.

O'Dea gave a bitter laugh. 'Two days,' he said. 'I have no food laid by. What with the bad weather, and the death of all the cattle, we have nothing to spare these days. This famine has hit us badly. I have no stocks at all and, what's worse: the well in the castle courtyard has been contaminated. We dare not drink the water from that. I've had men filling barrels from the river, but that won't last thirsty, fighting men for long. There's no getting away from our fate; I shouldn't have sent for you, O'Malachy. I should have left you to look after your own place in case the Normans move on to Drumshee once they have defeated us. We'll all die here like rats in a cellar.'

Like rats in a cellar, repeated Shane to himself as he walked his father's horse and his own towards the stables. He could see O'Dea's men coming back from the river carrying the heavy barrels – five men to each barrel – four to carry the barrel and one to hold the torch aloft. The ground around the river was so waterlogged that they could not risk the horses and carts there and the men were struggling and swearing under the weight of the water-filled oak barrels. From time to time, one of the men would slip and then the other three would have to put down the barrel and pull him out of the marshy ground. At this rate, they would not get much water into the castle before dawn. Suddenly an idea flashed into Shane's head and he turned away from the stables and followed his father and O'Dea towards the castle door.

'O'Dea,' he said. To his annoyance, the excitement made his voice high and child-like. He cleared his throat and started again. 'O'Dea, is there any way that we can get de Clare and his Norman knights to come through that marshy ground? Their horses will never manage to get through it and we could sally forth from the castle and fight them on foot.'

O'Dea shook his head. 'No, lad,' he said. 'They won't come that way. We've had word that they're camped by Ruan. They'll cross the stream by the ford up there at Maccon's place and turn south towards the castle. There's good, dry, high ground that way.'

'Yes, but . . . if we could lure them . . .' said Shane. He stopped for a moment and tried to put his thoughts into words.

'O'Dea,' he said eventually fixing his burning blue eyes on the two men and trying to make them understand the vision in his mind. 'Do you remember the time when you took me hunting wild duck? You put me and Fergus hiding in the wood beyond Ballycullinan Lake. We had our bows and arrows and our throwing knives. Then you crept around to the far side of the lake and made a duck sound with your whistle. You were the decoy. The ducks all went for the decoy and Fergus and I could shoot them at our ease.'

O'Dea nodded. 'I see your meaning, boy,' he said clapping Shane on the shoulder. 'We let them have sight of us and lure them on to the marshy ground.'

'It might work,' said O'Malachy slowly. 'Dangerous, though.'

'Better a fight in the open than dying like rats in a cellar,' said Shane hotly.

'Won't they suspect, though?' asked O'Malachy. 'Won't they see that the ground won't bear them and their horses?'

'We'll go back as far as the ford,' said Shane. The excitement was welling up inside him. He felt as if he were on fire. His cheeks were burning despite the cold rain which continued to fall. 'We'll be waiting there for them and then when we see them coming we'll dash across the river and the rest of you will be hiding behind the trees – in that little wood beyond the marshy ground.'

'Would they guess it was a trap?' asked O'Dea doubtfully.

'Perhaps we could be driving a small herd of cattle across the river,' said Shane eagerly. 'Then they'd assume that we were trying to get the cattle into the safety of the bawn inside the castle walls.'

'It might work,' said O'Neilan. 'It's worth trying.'

'And their horses will start to stick in the mud once they're over the river so they'll be easy prey for us,' said Con O'Donoghue. 'Well done, young Shane,' he added slapping Shane on the back. 'Where did he get the brains from, O'Malachy? Must be from his mother.'

O'Malachy scowled and shook his fist, and then grinned, but his eyes remained anxious. He turned towards Conor O'Dea.

'Who . . .?' he began.

'I'll do it,' interrupted Shane, 'let me do it. It's my idea. I know exactly what to do.'

'Not you, Shane,' said Conor O'Dea quickly. 'Not you, Shane, on the river! It's a good plan, but you're very young yet, and you are your father's only son. He's getting old now; he can't do without you. You'll stay in the trees with us. We'll put a few experienced old fellows like O'Donoghue on the river ford.'

Shane said nothing. He waited until his father stumped up the steps of the castle to catch a few hours' sleep in front of the fire and then he turned to O'Dea.

'O'Dea,' he said urgently. 'Let me be in the decoy party. You haven't any men that know that ground as well as I do. You know that. You know the hours that I have spent hunting wild birds down by the lake there. I'll be quite safe. You can be sure of that.'

'What if you get an arrow in your back? What do I say to your father then?' asked O'Dea grimly.

'Look at this jerkin,' said Shane proudly throwing open his cloak and showing the padded seams of the gleaming leather. 'My mother got this made for me. That's made from the hide of a bull – hard as iron, that leather – and each one of these seams is packed with a pound of mountain sheep's wool. No arrow could get through that.'

'Perhaps not our arrows,' said O'Dea uneasily, 'but the Normans have those longbows – the arrows come hard and fast from them.'

'You're turning into an old woman,' teased Shane, flinging an affectionate arm around the young man's shoulders. 'Let's go down and look at the ground near the ford over the river. I bet I can find the drier bits even by the light of a torch.'

'Leave it now,' shouted O'Dea to the men who were still struggling with the barrels of water. 'Let this be your last load. Go and dry off. There's a good fire blazing in the Great Hall. Get yourself warm and dry and rested. The attack will come soon after dawn.'

'You're going to do my plan, then?' asked Shane.

'It's our only chance,' said O'Dea briefly. 'Look there's the river. If they were coming across from Ruan to Dysart O'Dea they would cross the river at this ford here.'

'That's right,' said Shane, trying to make his voice sound deep and man-like, but then it cracked and rose high again as his excitement mounted. 'And if they were to go on to the castle, then the ground would be high and reasonably firm for their horses. So we need to turn them away from the good ground. What we need is to have everyone on foot – you and your men in the wood there hidden by the trees, my father and his men in the patch of bushes further north beside the lake so that they can come out behind them, and then me and a few men driving the herd of cows across the river over towards the woodland. They'll follow us.'

Without waiting for an answer, Shane splashed

into the ford and strode across the river.

'Look, we'll lead them over here, and you'll come out of the bushes there and attack, my father and his men will come in from behind and cut them off and then I'll turn my men and the cows over towards . . . yes, that's what I was looking for; there's a few yards of rock under the surface here – I've often stood here while I was waiting for the wild duck to fly. We'll bring the cows over here and then I'll join you.'

'It's a good plan,' said O'Dea grimly. 'But how are you going to explain it to your father when we go back to the castle now?'

'I won't be coming back with you,' said Shane airily. 'Lend me young Brian O'Hogan over there. He's a great runner. We'll go along the road to Ruan. Brian lives out that way; he knows that road as well as I know the roads around Drumshee. It must be well past midnight now. The Normans will be stirring in a few hours – the nights are short at this time of year. I'll send him back to you with a message when we hear the sound of them on the move and then you can have everything in place. You won't want the cows down there too early in case they wander. Say nothing about it to my father, tell him that I'm with Brian O'Hogan and will join you in the morning. We'll all be laughing about this by tomorrow night.'

Chapter 3

Fidelma's eyes followed the horsemen as they splashed through the ford and then climbed the hill opposite to Drumshee. When Shane had finally disappeared, she was left to turn back and go indoors and join her mother in the solar. *S438011*.

'He'll be all right,' she said as her mother raised a tear-stained face. 'Father will look after him.'

'I know,' said her mother. She dabbed her face with a square of soft linen and tried to smile. 'You know me,' she said. 'I cry easily. I was just thinking what he was like as a baby and how sweet he was. You couldn't keep him out of anything then – he even got out into the stables when he was still crawling. He was always the same. Never knew the meaning of fear. You were different. You were a little worrier – do you remember how frightened of spiders you used to be?'

Fidelma smiled. 'I remember when I was about six and I was scared because there seemed to be strange shadows in my room. I thought they were giant spiders. I screamed and Shane came running in with his little sword and pretended to stab them all to

21

death. I was quite happy then. I remember that he even threw the dead shadows out of the window.'

'He was always so brave,' said her mother softly, but then her face crumpled up and she began to sob noisily. 'I don't know what's to become of us all,' she said, the words almost lost in the noise of her weeping. 'These are terrible times. Your father may get killed. There are no rents coming in these days. The weather is so dreadful. It has done nothing but rain for the last six months. All the cattle are dying and there is famine in the land. We might have to leave this castle and go and live in a small cabin. There is no money to keep this castle up. We need silver to pay our servants and to buy goods.'

Fidelma nodded. She had heard all of this before, but somehow it did not seem real to her. She could not imagine living anywhere except in the castle at Drumshee. Money had never seemed to be short before. She and her mother had the finest and most fashionable gowns; Shane had his horse, his hawk, his velvet tunics and silken hose. The castle and the stables were full of servants. Life was good for them all.

'If only the weather would improve and the Normans go back to England,' said her mother. Again she dabbed her face with the square of linen, and then added. 'You go to bed now. All we can do is pray for them. Nothing will happen tonight. It's a black night. De Clare and his Normans won't move until dawn.'

Fidelma slept very little that night and when dawn broke early on this May morning she got out of bed and dressed herself quickly. She opened the shutters of the small window high above the ground and looked out. The rain had gone and the sun was just rising above the hill opposite. There was no sound from anywhere and there was no smoke from the small cabins around the castle. No one was up, but she.

I'll go out, she thought. I'll take Shane's hawk and let it fly. At least I can do that for him. Quickly she ran down the stairs, tugged open the big oak door and went across the courtyard to the stables.

The stables seemed very quiet without the two stallions. The farm horses were all dozing, her mother's mare stood quietly, though her head turned as soon as Fidelma came in, and Fidelma's pony, Brideen, whinnied a welcome.

'Yes, I'm still here,' said Fidelma kissing the pony's soft nose. 'Girls can't go out to fight. Let's put your bridle on and now your saddle.'

That was the easy part. Brideen stood very still; waiting calmly while Fidelma went over to the back of the stables for the hawk. Fidelma was a little afraid of this hawk. She had flown him before but she was not completely at ease when that savage yellow eye looked into hers. Her father had promised her a small hawk, a merlin, but Fidelma had been secretly glad when the money troubles had prevented him keeping his promise.

'Come on, Angus,' she murmured. The hawk was hooded so she stretched the long leather gauntlet over her left hand before lifting the hawk from his perch. She tied the soft leather straps, the jesses, to her wrist before she dared remove the hood. He sat calmly on her wrist and made no angry movements so she climbed up on Brideen and moved off through the courtyard.

'You're up early,' said old Brian coming yawning out of his cabin built under the southwest side of the enclosure. 'Take care of that hawk,' he added pulling open the iron gate to allow her to pass through. 'He's a funny fellow, that hawk, he only trusts Shane.'

'He'll be all right,' said Fidelma. She was used to hiding her feelings, used to pretending to a courage, which was not in her. She cantered down the long avenue and turned up towards Drumevin. When she came to the top of the hill, she wheeled her horse around and sat facing the castle with her back to the sun.

I'll throw the hawk towards the castle, she thought. Then, even if he doesn't come back to me, he'll fly back to the stables.

Gently she undid the jesses and tossed the hawk into the air. He rose high into the sky and seemed to remain there, motionless, surveying the small hills, the valley where the River Fergus ran fast and deep, the tall grey castle of Drumshee, and then, quite suddenly, he wheeled around and flew east towards Dysart O'Dea.

'Oh, no,' cried Fidelma. 'He is going to join Shane.'

I should never have flown him, she thought as she clapped her heels to Brideen's sides. Shane had told her that hawks have wonderful eyesight. Perhaps the hawk had seen the battle going on four miles away, perhaps he had even seen Shane and gone to join him. If he landed on Shane's wrist at the moment of battle he might be the cause of death to her brother.

'Angus, Angus,' she screamed frantically whirling the lure of magpie feathers around and praying that Angus, as he had been trained to do, would come back at the sight of the lure. Shane had spent many hundreds of hours whirling that lure and then rewarding the bird with a piece of meat. Surely it would not fail now. Desperately Fidelma galloped up the hill with the lure still whirling and dancing in the air.

When she reached the top of the long hill, Fidelma paused to allow Brideen to catch her breath. She was now on the moorland at the ancient boundary between Thomond and Corcomroe.

Dysart O'Dea was only two miles away to the east. The wind was to her back, blowing from the west so she could hear nothing from the battlefield. There was no sign of the hawk either. He would undoubtedly be at Dysart O'Dea by now. A hawk could fly at sixty miles an hour; he would be with Shane two minutes after he left her. She wondered whether she could go nearer but she knew she should not. She dared not go near. The Normans might capture her, take her prisoner, might do terrible things to her. She shivered and turned her pony's head towards home.

And then something made her turn her head. The sun was in her eyes, but a black shape with wide outstretched wings and curved tail came between her and the sun. She shielded her eyes with her right hand and almost as soon as she had done that her gauntleted left wrist felt the weight of the bird. Angus had come back. With trembling fingers she tied the jesses and slipped the hood over his savage yellow eyes.

But all the time that her fingers were busy, her mind insistently kept repeating these words:

He went to Shane. Why did he come back?

Angus would never leave Shane to come back to her!

Was Shane still alive?

Chapter 4

'Better put our torches out now,' said Shane putting his mouth close to Brian's ear so that his voice was just a soft murmur. 'We might be coming near to the camp.' He leaned over and thrust the tip of his pitch-burning torch into the watery ditch beside them. Brian did the same. The two torches fizzled briefly and then went out. The blackness was unbroken now and still the rain fell heavily.

'The word that we got was that they were right over as far as Ruan,' said Brian in the same hushed voice. 'If we could find some shelter here we could wait until dawn. We're just above the valley road now. They'll have to go through that on their way to Dysart O'Dea.'

'This tree is about as good shelter as we'll get,' murmured Shane. 'We won't risk going too far away from the road. As soon as we catch sight of them we'll be off. I'll wait by the river and you get back to the castle. O'Dea will be waiting for you with the herd of cows.'

The next couple of hours seemed long to Shane,

he blew on his fingers, stamped his feet, brushed the water from the thick, curled nap of his cloak and longed for the morning to come and the action to begin. Brian was curled up in a ball under the tree snoring lightly, but Shane was too excited to rest. A hundred, two hundred times, he tramped up and down under the shelter of the overhanging oak tree and then suddenly he stopped. In the distance towards Ruan was a sudden flash of light, then another, then another. Cautiously, he shook Brian awake and then clapped a hand over his mouth.

'Hush,' he said in his ear. 'They may have men out watching us, while we're watching them. Their fires have been uncovered. They'll be breakfasting and then they'll be on the move.'

The two boys stood side-by-side watching. Dawn would soon be here. The deep blackness of the night had faded to a pale grey. The rain had stopped, but mist rose up from the soaked land.

'Fog,' whispered Brian.

'Pray not,' returned Shane in his ear. 'That will ruin all our plans. They must be able to see us lead the cattle across the ford.'

But as they watched their hearts sank. It was indeed a thick fog. After all this rain a fog rising from the drenched ground, on a wind-less day like this, could last all day.

'They're on the move,' said Brian. 'They're carrying torches.'

Down below from where they stood they could see a long line of mounted horsemen beginning to move along the track. Every horseman carried a torch of burning pitch. The light glinted on their swords and on their mail coats of knitted iron links.

'Run!' said Shane vehemently. 'Get back to the castle as quickly as you can. You know your way; they don't. They'll have to go slowly with their horses in this poor light. Tell O'Dea to get his men and my father's men into position. They'll have to move without torches, but tell him to give torches to the decoy party and to the men with the cows. We'll turn this fog to our own advantage.

Chapter 5

In a moment Brian was off, his bare feet making little sound as he ran down the path. Shane followed him, but he was slower. This road to Ruan was not so well known to him as it was to Brian. From time to time he stopped and listened. He could hear the sounds from behind him, the clop, clop of horses' hoofs, the ring of metal sword striking metal coat, the high whinny of excitement from a stallion. The sounds did not grow nearer, though. He was managing to keep ahead of them. It was, as he had guessed: De Clare and his Norman knights were finding it hard to follow the rough track through the dense white fog that covered all landmarks. Their torches would be of little use to them, Shane surmised, but he prayed that they would keep them alight. Not only he, but also O'Dea and all his men, would see this army approaching the O'Dea territory.

However, as they came down towards the river, suddenly an order rang out; all torches were immediately quenched. Shane felt himself quite disoriented. While the torches had been behind him, he had felt confident that he was going in the right direction but now he was not sure. He could not tell how near he was to the river. He hesitated; if he stumbled into the river in full flood he might drown. In an agony of despair he bit the back of his hand fiercely. He could not let down O'Dea and O'Malachy; everyone was depending on him. He made a quick decision. He would keep running. Some instinct would guide him.

Then just ahead of him came salvation. Someone had lit a torch! Brian must have got back to the castle. The light of the torch was muffled by the white sogginess of the choking fog, but it was enough. That was the ford. Shane's long legs moved even faster. In a couple of minutes he would be with them. On this day, 18th May 1318, he would prove himself worthy of the name of O'Malachy.

He was not the only one to see the torch. From behind him came a shout of triumph. The Normans had seen the light. They were quite near to him now. They were spurring on their horses. The noise of the hoofs was getting louder. Then there was a scream of a horse and a wild shriek from a man. Someone had stumbled and fallen over the rocky edge of the track. There was a shouted command and the noise of the horses slowed down again. Shane kept running and he did not look back. Now he could see that the torch was held by Brian, breathless and sweating, but with a grin from ear to ear across his freckled face.

'Sure, what took you so long,' he said teasingly. 'We've been waiting for you to start the fun.'

There were ten men there – armed with short swords and protected by leather jerkins. Each one of them was carrying an unlit torch. Behind them there was a small herd of wild-looking bullocks; some lads armed with cudgels, and behind them a small company of archers.

'Light all the torches,' shouted Shane.

Then ten torches flared up through the fog. The white air turned golden. From behind came a shout, the French rallying cry.

'*À moi!*' screamed de Clare, and the Normans swept on towards the ford their horses' hoofs crashing and sparking on the gravel-filled track.

'O'Dea, *abú!*' shouted Shane, and the other men-at-arms took up the cry and began to drive the herd of cattle across the ford. The small company of Irish archers did not follow, however. They took up their position on the bank of the ford and turned to fire at the on-coming Normans.

'Don't fire!' shouted Shane. For one moment he

despaired. His plan was going to fail. O'Dea had probably told the archers to guard the backs of the men driving the cattle. But what would be the use of them firing now? They had to lure as many of the enemy as possible across the river before any move was made. Eagerly he scanned the Norman troops. There was de Clare, himself; he could see his banner floating in the light of the torches.

'Cross the river, everyone,' he shouted. The Normans might not understand his language but they would understand the gesture of his frantically waving arms. There might even be one or two who would understand Gaelic.

'Hold your fire,' he screamed again to the archers. 'Let's get inside the castle walls, first.'

And then they were across the ford and he had guided the cattle on to the solid rocky ground. O'Dea's archers were still covering their retreat with their bow-and-arrows, but not a shot had been fired. Shane held his breath. Would his plan work?

And then de Clare himself and six of his knights were in the river. Their horses moved quickly through the shallow waters of the ford and then up the bank and onto the soft ground. From the corner of his eye, Shane saw O'Malachy and his thirty men move out from the trees behind him and, just ahead of him, O'Dea and a company of twenty men, all brandishing swords, jumped out of the willows around the lake.

Now the Normans were lost. Their heavy horses, burdened down by riders in chain mail, plunged and stuck in the wet marshy ground. Swords flashed and in an instant before Shane's dazzled eyes, de Clare and his six knights lay dead on the ground. For a moment, the rest of the Normans hesitated on the far side of the river and then a young voice shouted: '*À moi!*' and plunged his horse into the ford. A young man, dressed in armour, splashed through the river, picked up the banner that had been dropped and waved it. For a moment Shane saw the banner of gold, emblazoned with three red chevrons, wave over the young man's head and then he himself was engulfed in a crowd of plunging, rearing horses and stabbing swords.

His own sword had been blooded now. He neither saw nor cared who had been killed. It was like living a dream: stab, recoil, defend, and attack. They were outnumbered; he could see that. But the Irish were on their own legs on the ground; the Normans were mounted on horses that could make no progress against this sticky mud and marshland. The young man with the banner had now fallen heavily from his horse and lay there stunned. O'Malachy approached him, sword in hand and stood over him.

'No, Father!' screamed Shane. He had slain Normans himself this morning and he would go on slaying them, but somehow he could not see this heroic young man killed in cold blood, killed when he could do nothing to shield himself. 'No, father,' he shouted, pulling the young knight aside. 'Keep him. We might be able to use him for barter if one of our own is captured. He may be de Clare's son.'

Before his father could reply, Shane bent down and pulled the young man over towards the bushes. The red and gold banner he left on the ground; the young man would get no protection from it now.

Then he was back into the battle. They were beginning to get the worse of it now. The Normans had regrouped under an older and more experienced leader. The horses had been abandoned and they fought hand-to-hand in a tight, disciplined formation. These were well-trained soldiers, not just men with swords in their hands. Their archers, too, with their longbows, were drawn up in a tight group on the far side of the ford and were firing steadily at the Irish. O'Quinn was on the ground now and his two sons with him; O'Brien, O'Lochlan, they all died at the hands of the Normans. Shane fought like a tiger; he allowed no feeling of despair or terror come to him, but he knew that the odds were against the O'Dea and O'Malachy clans.

And then a great shout came from the hill towards the west.

'O'Conor, *abú!*' was the shout that came down to the weary clansmen fighting a force of three times their own number. Shane stopped for a moment, sword raised in the air. The fog was now clearing and the golden sunshine coloured the horsemen making their way down the hill. It was Felim O'Conor of Corcomroe; Shane could see the huge man on his enormous grey stallion. He must have fifty men with him! Now they could win!

Shane turned back to the battle with new determination in his heart. But it was too late. That second of inattention, of inexperience, perhaps, had doomed him. A sword plunged into his right arm, knocking his own sword from his nerveless grip. In a moment, he was on the ground and staring up into a merciless helmeted face.

And that was when a hawk, with savage yellow eyes, swooped down between them.

Chapter 6

18th May 1318

Like carded clouds of white sheep's wool, wrote Fidelma. She was trying to concentrate on writing her poem, trying to keep her mind off the battle that would now be raging over at Dysart O'Dea. She looked out through the open window of the library at the misty valley and then at the cloud of purple bluebells under the pale green of the beech trees. It was no good, though. She could think of nothing but her brother and her father out there across the hills. Carefully she replaced her quill into the horn, filled with soot-black ink, left the library and joined her mother in the solar.

'Why are you wearing your new dress?' asked her mother irritably.

Fidelma did not answer. She found it hard to explain. When she had come back from her ride she had changed into her new dress in an effort to pretend that everything was well, and somehow the glowing crimson silk, the carefully knotted long silver girdle, the gold net, the crespine, enclosing her braided hair had helped her to believe that all would be well and that any minute now they would hear shouts of joy and triumph and Shane and her father would ride up the avenue.

'I'll go down to the stables,' she said hastily. 'I want to make sure that Shane's hawk is all right. I left him unhooded when I came back from the ride.'

Without waiting for an answer she went out of the door and down the stairs to the Great Hall. Some of the women servants were there, rubbing a mixture of beeswax and lavender into the hundred-year-old table and chairs and the heavy oak chests. They looked at her and she read the reflection of her own anxieties in their eyes. Each one of them had a father or husband or son out there across the hills at Dysart O'Dea.

The stables were dark and quiet but the light from the door outlined the hawk. He was not hooded, but his savage yellow eyes were closed and his head lay sunken on his breast. He looked like a bird that had given up on life. The sight of him made Fidelma shake. What had he seen this morning? Did he know something? Quickly she slipped the hood over his head. She had helped Shane make this hood out of leather with a cluster of bright feathers from a jay decorating the top. She felt better when the drooping head and the dull eyes were hidden beneath it.

It was at that moment that she heard a sound. Surely that was the noise of horsemen? Perhaps they were coming home in triumph. She ran out of the stables, crossed the courtyard and tugged open the iron gates, pushing back the hood of her cloak so that she could see better. Yes, they were coming. But there was no triumph in those horsemen. They rode slowly and soberly. She narrowed her eyes in an effort to pick out and give name to the figures riding three abreast behind their leader. There was O'Malachy himself at the head of his men; she knew him by his bulk and by the dappled grey of his stallion. So he was safe. The heads of all the horsemen behind him were bowed so it was difficult to tell who they were. Automatically she began to count; thirty horsemen had rode out behind her father. Had thirty come back?

Three, six, nine, twelve, fifteen, eighteen, twenty-one, twenty-four, twenty-seven, thirty. She turned to Old Brian who had followed her out of the stables.

'They're all there!' she exclaimed. A rush of warmth and of excitement ran through her veins. Quickly she undid the ribbon around her neck and swung the heavy cloak from her shoulders, placed it in his hands, and then she began to run down the avenue as rapidly as she could.

She was at the end of the avenue before

O'Malachy reached it. He stopped at the sight of her. There was no joy, no triumph in his face. He opened his mouth and then shut it and went on up the avenue. Then came O'Donoghue, O'Neilan, and all the rest of them. In the last row came Mort Queally and his son who was holding the bridle of a magnificent black stallion with a tall, slim young man sitting on it. It was Shane's stallion, but it was not Shane on the horse; this was a young man dressed in coat of mail with the hood hanging down at his back, a blond boy with brown eyes that widened at the sight of her.

And his hands were tied in front of him.

* * *

'He was on the ground,' said O'Malachy heavily. Suddenly he seemed an old man as he looked at the white faces of his wife and of his daughter. The prisoner had been locked in the cellar; the men had gone back to their farms. At Dysart O'Dea they would all be celebrating the defeat of the Normans; here at Drumshee there could be no cheer, no feast, no celebrations of the victory; Shane, the young heir to Drumshee, had not come home. And now his family stood alone in the Great Hall.

'I thought he was gone,' continued O'Malachy, forcing the words out. 'I was sure that he had been stabbed. I . . . I couldn't see for a moment, but then I heard a shout from the man who took over when de Clare was killed – I don't know what he said . . . I blinked and then I saw the body . . .' he gulped and then corrected himself, 'I saw Shane being slung across the back of a horse and led away. I was on top of the hill looking down . . . and then I lost sight of them.'

He stopped and looked at his wife and the tears in his eyes mirrored hers. He put his hand out and took her hand.

'Con O'Donoghue swears that Shane was still alive,' he said earnestly. 'His sword arm had been injured, O'Donoghue saw the blood dripping from him, but he says that Shane's eyes looked back at him and that he was still alive.'

'If he is alive, we can get him back,' said his wife resolutely. 'Is that why you took the young Norman knight as a prisoner?'

O'Malachy nodded. 'Yes, it's almost as if Shane could see into the future. He was the one who persuaded me to spare the young fellow's life. He may be someone important, Shane said. He was the one who snatched up the banner after de Clare fell dead. I'll go and see him now. I wanted to tell you first.'

'Why don't you get Donogh to bring him up

here,' said Fidelma. 'Treat him well; he can't escape from here.'

'He's a prisoner,' said her father briefly. 'He can't expect better.'

'Treat him as you hope that someone else will treat Shane,' said his daughter bravely. O'Malachy glared at her, but Fidelma turned to her mother.

'We'll learn more if we treat him with respect,' she said and her mother nodded.

'Bring him up, Donal,' she said. 'He can help us to send a message. If he speaks no Gaelic then Fidelma can speak French to him. Most of these Normans speak French, they say.'

O'Malachy stumped across the floor and pulled open the door of the little room leading to the kitchen and bawled out: 'Donogh, fetch the prisoner.'

They were in the hall in a moment, small round redheaded Donogh and the prisoner, tall as Shane, but with blond hair and brown eyes. His eyes went immediately to Fidelma and looked intently at her, but then turned back to her father.

'Do you speak Gaelic?' asked O'Malachy roughly.

The boy shook his head and threw out his hands to show that he did not understand, but he did not speak. Once again his brown eyes went to Fidelma. They moved over the coils of rich brown hair netted in the gold crespine, then down the crimson, close-fitting dress with its silver girdle, down to the laced brown shoes, and then back to her face. Quite unexpectedly, he smiled and swept her a low bow. Fidelma flushed.

'Question him, Fidelma,' said O'Malachy.

'Where do you come from?' asked Fidelma trying to remember the right words. A year ago Father Simon had come over from France to found the Augustine Abbey at Kilshanny. He had stayed for some months at Drumshee while the abbey was being built and he had taught French to both Shane and Fidelma.

The blond young man bowed again. 'I come from Limerick,' he said. 'My name is Hugh de Barry. My stepfather is the constable at King John's castle at Limerick. King John was the grandfather of the present king, King Edward II.'

'No king of ours,' growled O'Malachy when Fidelma had translated the reply. 'Ask him about Shane.'

Fidelma turned back. 'My brother has been carried away, injured, perhaps . . .' she stopped but forced herself to go on, '. . . perhaps, dead. Did you see what happened? Do you know who took him?'

'It was one of my stepfather's men,' replied Hugh.

'My stepfather did not go with de Clare to the battle as he was ill with the ague. He sent me in his place, I didn't do very well,' he added rather bitterly.

'Do you think that your stepfather will exchange you for my brother Shane?' asked Fidelma.

'I'm sure that he will,' said Hugh confidently. 'After all,' he continued, 'I am the heir to the de Barry property in Cork. When I reach eighteen that estate will be mine. My stepfather is but the guardian to that property now.'

'Is your mother alive?' asked Fidelma.

'No,' replied Hugh, 'I and my sister Isabelle and my little brother Giles all live with my stepfather at King John's castle in Limerick.'

'What is he saying, Fidelma?' asked O'Malachy impatiently.

'He thinks that his stepfather will exchange him for Shane,' said Fidelma briefly.

'How will we get in touch?' mused O'Malachy.

'What about Father Simon?' asked Fidelma. It was a surprise to her to hear herself suggesting, leading the way, she who was usually so silent. Suddenly she seemed filled with courage. 'He could easily go. There is St Peter's, the Augustine abbey in Limerick. If you sent a couple of men and a horse for him he would surely go.' She stopped and swallowed and then found the words to go on. 'He loves Shane as everyone does,' she continued quietly. 'He would not allow a hair of his head to be injured if he could prevent it in anyway.'

'We'll do it first thing tomorrow morning,' said O'Malachy jumping to his feet like a man who is bursting for some action. 'Father Simon will be able to explain to this Norman that we hold his stepson and that we will exchange him unharmed for Shane.'

'Better still, get this boy to write a letter saying that he is unharmed and that he wishes this exchange to take place,' suggested his wife.

'Will you write a letter explaining everything to your stepfather?' asked Fidelma.

'Gladly,' said Hugh with another one of his courtly bows.

'I'll take him up to the library,' said Fidelma. 'We'll write the letter there. I'll give him pen and ink and vellum.'

'Donogh must go with you and make sure that he does not try to escape,' said O'Malachy. 'He has no knife or anything, Donogh, does he?'

'Nothing,' said Donogh. 'Do I take him back to the cellar when they're finished with this letter?'

Fidelma looked at her mother. She knew how cold and damp the cellar was. After these months of rain it was even damper than ever. 'I hope Shane is not in a cellar,' she said quietly with her eyes still fixed on her mother's face.

'He can sleep in that inner room beside the Great Hall,' declared O'Malachy after a short moment when the struggle within him showed clearly in his face. 'Donogh, you must sleep beside him and call for help if anything happens.'

Fidelma smiled. The heat of the chimney in the Great Hall warmed the small room. The young Norman would sleep comfortably there.

'Get the key, Donogh,' she said, and while they waited for Donogh to return, she explained in careful French, 'We always keep the library door locked as my great-grandfather filled it with very precious books.'

The young Norman nodded, his brown eyes warm and filled with admiration. 'I love books,' he said. 'My mother had a book of poetry and she used to read it to Isabelle and myself when we were young. I loved listening to her. She had a voice like you have.'

Fidelma blushed slightly. Donogh had returned and had gone ahead of them. She and Hugh followed him up the spiral staircase towards the library on the third floor. 'This is our library,' she said pushing open the door.

'Magnificent,' murmured Hugh looking all around him at the shelves and cupboards holding hundreds of books. 'King John's castle has nothing as fine as this.'

'Here is a sheet of vellum and a pen,' said Fidelma, quickly snatching away her earlier attempts at a poem and hastily stuffing the sheets into the small chest on the table.

Hugh sat down and dipped his pen in the ink so vigorously that some small blots flew out and scattered all over the page. 'Good,' he said happily. 'Now my stepfather will know it is mine. He has often beaten me for my untidiness and lack of scholarship. Well, now for the letter.'

He was no scholar, even if he did like books, thought Fidelma with a smile on her lips. The pen in his hand was as awkward to him as a sword would be to her. It took him a long time to write the few simple words and the leaf of vellum was scored with crossings out and decorated with blobs and blots of ink. In the end the letter was finished and she carefully blotted it with some fine sea sand.

'We'll give this to Father Simon in the morning,' she said rising to her feet.

'Wait a minute,' said Hugh seizing a small piece of vellum trimmed from the leaf and left lying on the table. 'Wait a minute; I want to write something else.'

This time he wrote quickly with no mistakes, no crossings out, and no blots. There were just four words on the piece of vellum when he held it out to her.

Donogh craned his head forwards but he would not be able to read French so Fidelma just looked away and pretended not to look at the words. She had read them, though.

'*Vous êtes très belle.*' You are very beautiful, the strange young Norman had written.

And suddenly she did feel beautiful.

And then she felt guilty that this pleasure, this excitement could be hers while she still did not know the fate of the brother who was so dear to her.

 # Chapter 7

To Shane, it seemed an eternity. But perhaps it was less than a second. The Norman face, its head encased in the iron helmet, stared into his and the man's sword was raised aloft. Shane shut his eyes; then resolutely he opened them. Images of Drumshee, his father, his mother, and his sister all floated through his mind. He stared intently at the sword descending towards his breast.

And then suddenly, just as a stone drops from a high window, a hawk dropped out of the sky, came between him and the Norman soldier and then landed on Shane's left arm. Shane felt the talons grip his wrist.

'*Mon Dieu!*' swore the soldier. He jumped back as if he had seen an evil spirit and then swiped his sword at Angus. With an angry cry, Angus rose up, flapped his wings once, and flew back towards Drumshee. Shane's eyes followed him longingly.

'Don't kill that young fellow,' roared another voice. 'Look at his clothes. He's the son of a chief. They've got young de Barry, the constable's stepson.

Take this boy to the back of the lines. We'll exchange him later on when we've beaten them.'

So Shane found himself hoisted on to the back of a horse. By now he was almost fainting with the pain of his wounded right arm. He dimly sensed that they were going back through the battle lines. They were not the only ones retreating. He was aware of that. It looked as if many of the Norman knights had turned their backs and started to flee. There were shouts of triumph from the Irish side. Felim O'Connor of Corcomroe had arrived; Shane had seen that for himself, but now it sounded as if there was another clan arriving from the south. It must be O'Hehir of Magowna.

Shane, like Fidelma, had learned French. Nevertheless, he found it difficult to understand what the soldiers were shouting. Many of them spoke English, or a mixture of French and English. But there was one word that he caught: Limerick. He knew Limerick; it was a city about forty miles from Drumshee. His mother had been fostered by a family who lived near there. He had gone there often when he was younger and had looked across the River Shannon at the huge castle with its towers and its thirty-feet-high walls around it. They were taking him to Limerick castle and they would keep him there. He would be a prisoner; perhaps he would die like a rat in a cellar after all, he thought. Then the pain became too much for him to bear and he fainted.

From time to time during the thirty-mile journey to Limerick Shane awoke to consciousness. He was aware that the horse had stopped once and that his arm had been roughly bound to stop the bleeding and then again, that he had been lifted from the back of the horse, and placed in a cart. He slept then for some time and only woke when the cart had stopped. This must be Limerick, he thought, but the pain of his wounded arm was still so bad that he kept his eyes shut.

'Bunratty!' he heard. And then the shock in one of the Norman's voices. 'O'Brien has burned Bunratty castle out.'

So Murrough O'Brien, O'Dea's overlord, had burned de Clare's stronghold. Surely the Normans were being driven back east across the Shannon. Perhaps the Irish would even regain Limerick at some time. The thought gave him courage. His arm had stopped bleeding, he realised. It would heal. He was young and strong. Perhaps he might be able to escape; perhaps even O'Brien and his men would march on Limerick. Shane's temperament always led him to expect the best. The sun always shone for him! Smiling to himself, he closed his eyes and settled himself to sleep for the last few miles of the journey.

It was raining again by the time that they reached Limerick. The heavy rain on his face woke Shane. He raised himself cautiously on his left elbow and stared around curiously. The cart was rattling across a stone bridge that had been built across a wide river. This was the River Shannon. Beyond it was King John's castle. Shane's heart sank when he saw it. He had forgotten how big it was. This castle was enormous.

King John's castle was built on a small island beside the river. It had six huge towers all joined together by a wall. The top of the wall and the tops of the six towers were crenellated – the up-and-down pattern of stones allowed archers to stand protected from the attackers, but able to dart in and out of cover to fire arrows at them. The river circled three sides of the castle; the only way in was across the bridge to the twin gate towers and even then a small ditch or drain formed a yawning gap between the road and the gate.

The horsemen and the carts all paused outside the gate towers. Shane could hear a shout – some sort of password, he thought. Then the portcullis was winched up, the creaks sounding loud in the evening air. Next a wooden bridge was lowered down over the ditch and the heavy gates were swung open. First the horsemen galloped in, then the carts with the wounded trundled after them.

Shane lay quietly, knowing that there was nothing he could do now. The look of the great castle frightened him. Would any of the Irish clans, even the most war-like of them all, ever be able to get past defences such as these?

'And who is this?' asked a voice. Bending over the cart was a man hugely fat and dressed in a long gown of fine silk covered over with a furred cloak. 'This is not one of our men,' he went on.

'No, my Lord Constable,' said the Norman captain coming across. 'One of the men was going to kill him, but I shouted to him to hold off. My Lord, I have ill news for you. Your stepson, Hugh de Barry, has been taken prisoner.'

'Was he killed?' asked the fat man hastily.

'No, no,' said the captain. 'Your Lordship would have been proud of him. He bravely snatched up de Clare's banner when de Clare fell, murdered by those savages. He was taken prisoner by the Irish so when I saw that we would be defeated I took this young fellow back with us so that we could barter him for your stepson. He is the son of one of their chiefs, I would say. Look at his clothes. His shirt is silk and his tunic is velvet. The surcoat is of the finest leather.'

This was even better than Shane had hoped. This Hugh de Barry must be the young man he had saved from O'Malachy's sword. If this were true, Shane would soon be on his way back to Drumshee. He would be ransomed. He and the young Norman would be exchanged at some halfway place between Drumshee and Limerick. What could be a better end to the adventure? Shane stared curiously at the fat man. For a moment he could have sworn that a look of disappointment had crossed the Lord Constable's face. Perhaps he had hoped to hang the prisoner and now he was going to have to return him unharmed.

'Lock him up in the cellar of the Constable's Tower,' shouted the fat man after a long moment and then he strode off to look at the rest of the wounded.

'You'd think he would have thanked you,' said the man who had driven the cart.

'That's not his way,' said the captain briefly. 'Anyway, we'd better get a priest from St Peter's to look at his arm. If he dies, he won't be much good as ransom for young de Barry. You go off and find that priest, Father Thomas, who is so good at poulticing wounds and I'll get the boy lodged in the cellar.'

The cellar was dry and reasonably warm with an immense fireplace in it. Shane stared at it with surprise. It was definitely a fireplace – a fireplace with a huge iron basket to hold charcoal. He had never seen a cellar with a fireplace. Certainly neither the cellar at Dysart O'Dea castle nor at his father's castle in Drumshee held a fireplace. They were both cold, damp, dark places where barrels of wine and the odd captive could be stored.

'Speak French?' asked the captain seeing his look. Shane nodded.

'Well that makes life easier,' said the captain. 'This used to be the mint – they used to mint coins here in the time of King John. They would melt the silver here on the fire, pour it into moulds, turn them out onto this stone slab here and then stamp the king's head on them on this old table over here. No coin-making here now, but the fire basket remains. I'll get some charcoal brought down now and some straw to make a bed for you. You'll be comfortable enough here – better than out in the rain, anyway. I thought I'd die of cold camped out in the hills of Thomond.'

He seems friendly, thought Shane. 'I'll make sure that my father rewards you, too, when I am exchanged for your constable's stepson,' he said earnestly.

The man smiled. People always liked Shane. 'Let's hope it's soon for your sake,' he said. 'I'll go and get the charcoal first and then make up a bed for you.'

He was back in a few minutes with a leather bucket full of charcoal. He tumbled some into the iron basket, added some dry straw and then opened his tinderbox and struck a light. The straw blazed up and then the small coals glowed – first orange, then a deep crimson. Shane sat down on the ground beside it and leaned against the wall. His wound was making him feel sick and very cold, and the warmth of the fire was comforting to him.

'I'll get your bed now, but you must keep the straw away from the fire,' said the captain.

When he returned, with a straw mattress, a priest in a brown habit was with him. 'Here is Father Thomas,' he announced. 'He is from the Augustine abbey.'

'Some hot water, my son,' murmured the priest. He took a bundle from the breast of his habit and laid it on a stone slab on the floor. The captain went to the foot of the steps and shouted an order.

'We have an Augustinian abbey near us, at Kilshanny,' said Shane.

'Don't speak,' said the priest, 'your strength is low.'

He took a sharp knife from his bundle and slit the

silken sleeve of Shane's tunic. The wound was a bad one; Shane could see that at a glance. It looked as if the sword had almost severed a portion of the flesh of the upper arm.

'At least the bone doesn't seem to be injured,' said the priest, feeling cautiously around. 'Lift your arm as high as you can for me.'

Shane lifted the arm. The pain made him wince and gasp, but he was able to raise his arm above his head. The priest grunted with satisfaction.

'Yes,' he said. 'It's just a bad flesh wound. What we have to guard against now is infection and fevers. I'll put this paste of goosegrass on it. It's a green salve and heals wounds well.'

Shane laughed. 'Goosegrass!' he said. 'I remember that I used to put handfuls of that down my sister's neck when we were children. It used to stick inside her dress. I remember she used to scream!'

The priest smiled, but he said no more, and he made no sound as he moistened a piece of linen and then heaped the green paste on it and tied the linen pad to Shane's upper arm. Shane was sure that he made no sound and yet his sharp young ears caught the sound of a giggle, two giggles from the darkness behind him. He turned his head and stared. He could see nothing at first, but then the priest lifted the candle and moved it. The light fell on the steps, barely reaching to the top step.

And on the top step Shane could see the hem of a dress – a beautiful dress of white satin with gold embroidery, with two slippers peeping from under the hem of the dress, and beside the dress were a pair of fine leather shoes – not very big – and above them crimson hose.

There was a boy and a woman – or perhaps a girl – the giggles sounded young and light-hearted – standing on the top of the steps, listening. Who were they? What were they doing in this grim castle?

Chapter 8

The boy came to Shane's dungeon four days later.

Each day the priest, Father Thomas, came to dress Shane's arm. Usually one of the guards accompanied him and stood swinging the huge key while the wound was cleansed and new pads of linen, soaked in the green paste of goosegrass, were tied over it.

This day, however, the priest came alone. Shane heard him unlock the door, open it and then come heavily down the steps. However, there had been no noise of the lock turning again. A moment later the flame of the candle flickered and then there was the soft sound of a door opening and then closing over. Light footsteps trod warily down the steps and then more confidently as the owner of the footsteps could see that only the prisoner and the priest were in the cellar.

'Giles!' said Father Thomas with a guilty start. 'How did you get in here? Did I leave the key in the door?'

'Yes, Father,' said a young voice, and a boy, aged

about twelve, moved forward into the light. He was a blond boy with dark brown eyes. His face was sweet and innocent with a gently smiling mouth and round pink cheeks, but his brown eyes had a sparkle of mischief in them. In his hand he held a large iron key.

'I thought you might need some help,' he continued sweetly. 'I could fetch and carry for you. You know how interested I am in herbs and herbal remedies.'

'Are you, Giles?' asked the priest with the innocent astonishment of a man who would never tell a lie. 'Oh well, that's good. You never seem to be interested in your books, but perhaps this is different. You can help me to tend the prisoner's wound. Heat some water there over the fire and then we'll soak the cloths before taking them off.'

'Were you in the battle?' asked Giles eagerly, as he poured some water from a flask into the pot that hung over the fire.

'Yes,' said Shane smiling. He guessed that the battle interested the boy more than herbs.

'Did you see my brother, Hugh?' asked Giles. 'He looks like me, but he's taller, of course.'

'Yes,' said Shane. 'Yes, I think I saw your brother. You are the stepson of the constable of the castle, then. I'm afraid that I don't know his name.'

The boy made a face. 'Old guzzle-guts,' he said disgustedly. 'That's a good enough name for him.'

'Now, Giles,' said Father Thomas. 'Sir John de Courcy is the constable of this castle,' he added to Shane.

'My name is de Barry,' said Giles. 'There are three of us: Hugh is the eldest, then there's Isabelle, she's just a girl, and then there's me, I'm the youngest. Hugh's lucky. When he's eighteen he can get away from this place and live at our father's castle in Cork.'

'Perhaps Hugh will let you live with him,' said Shane smiling.

'If he gets married – that's what Isabelle says.' Suddenly the boy's face changed. It crumpled and he turned his head away from Shane and bent over the pot. Shane noticed that the boy's hand shook as he poured the hot water into the priest's bowl. Still keeping his back turned to Shane, he said in a shaky voice: 'Is Hugh still alive? Do you know? Has he been killed? He didn't come back with the others?'

'But haven't you heard?' asked Shane. He could hear the shock, and the astonishment, in his own voice, and the boy spun around quickly. 'Of course, he is still alive!' continued Shane. 'Haven't you heard?' he repeated. 'I am going to be ransomed for him.'

'Are you sure?' asked the boy doubtfully. 'I heard that rumour from the men in the barracks, but when I asked my stepfather, he told me that Hugh was probably dead. I'm sure that he wishes Hugh were dead. He wishes that we were all dead. I hate him!'

'Now, Giles,' said the priest nervously. He gave an anxious look at the stairs behind and then turned back. 'Let's have no more of this talk against Sir John,' he said firmly. 'If you are going to help me, then keep a still tongue in your head. Hold the bowl and let me soak the linen. Now we'll peel it away.'

'It looks very bad,' said Giles, flinching slightly.

'It's much better than it was,' said Shane calmly

The priest carried the old stained pad of linen over to the fire and dropped it in. It sizzled and then steamed. The fire was low and the wet pad made it smoke.

'I'll get a poker,' said Giles and bounded up the steps.

He was back in a few minutes carrying a large iron poker. Busily he poked the fire and then added some more charcoal. The flames leapt up and the white walls of the dark cellar turned orange with the light from the fire. Giles beat the lumps of charcoal enthusiastically, sending sparks flying.

'Let me do it,' scolded the priest.

Giles meekly handed the poker to him and then came over and knelt beside Shane.

'Your brother is a very brave man, I saw him snatch up the banner when de Clare let it fall,' said Shane speaking quietly under the noise which the priest was making with the poker. 'My father will hold him prisoner; he will not harm him.'

The boy smiled and the merry mischievous look came back into his eyes. Carefully he spread the green paste onto a clean linen pad and held it against Shane's arm while the priest wound a long strip around to keep it in place.

'I'll come again this evening,' said Father Thomas with his hand against Shane's forehead. 'I think you may have a slight fever. I'll bring you a herbal drink. I would bring it now, but I have to attend mass, and then I have a sermon to preach in a church across the town.'

'I'll bring it,' said Giles obligingly. He gave a quick wink at Shane when the priest turned away to put the wooden bowl back in his leather satchel, but his face was as innocent as a two-year-old's when the priest turned back. 'I can keep the key and then put it back in the gatehouse when I have given him the fever drink, Father Thomas. No one will even notice.'

'Do you think that would be all right?' asked the priest doubtfully.

'Of course,' said Giles cheerfully. 'I am trusted with everything around here.'

Not very likely, thought Shane, but he said nothing. He could understand that the boy wanted to know more about his brother. This Sir John did not appear to be much of a father to him.

'Well, perhaps it will do no harm,' said the priest. 'The sooner he gets this fever drink of willow leaves and bark, the faster he will recover. You can come across to the abbey with me, Giles, and bring it back. Your sister will show you how to heat it.'

Shane did feel quite unwell; he was beginning to discover. His head burned and his eyelids drooped. He hardly noticed the two going out and had sunk back onto his straw bed before the heavy door clanged shut.

★   ★   ★

For days it seemed to Shane that he lay there burning with fever. People came and went; his head was held up and some hot liquid was poured between his lips. Sometimes it was the priest, sometimes the captain of the guards, and sometimes young Giles. Once he fancied that it was his mother when a soft voice spoke in his ear and a soft hand was held over his burning forehead. And then he fell into an uneasy sleep. Scenes of the battle seemed to be going around and around in his head. He dreamt that his hawk was flying straight at O'Dea, the savage beak flashing like a sword, and then he woke with a cry.

'Hush,' said a voice in his ear. 'Here drink this.'

I must be still dreaming, thought Shane. He and Fidelma had some wonderful painted books that their great-grandfather Malachy had bought from France for the library at Drumshee. Now it seemed as if he had found his way into one of those books where beautiful ladies sat on bright green grass seats with flowers all around them. The face that bent over him was a face from one of those romances.

The face looking into his own was a perfect oval, the skin was alabaster fair with a red mouth, the eyes were the brown of sunlit, autumn leaves and the hair was a dark gold, braided and looped inside its fine golden net. It was a beautiful girl dressed in a gown of shimmering white satin embroidered with threads of gold.

'Drink,' said the voice again. 'I've heated it over the fire and put some spices from the east in it. You will soon feel better when you drink it. You have been in a fever.'

Obediently Shane drank. He did feel better. The

spiced hot drink cleared his head.

'Sweet,' he said with a wondering smile.

The beautiful face so near to his own blushed slightly. 'I've put honey in it,' she said, and her own voice was as smooth and as sweet as honey.

'Oh, the drink,' said Shane and then he smiled. He had never seen a girl as beautiful as this Norman girl. 'Your hair is the colour of rich gold,' he said admiringly.

'He's raving,' said Giles peeping over the shoulder of his sister. 'A while ago he was raving about hawks and now he's raving about your hair.'

'He's quite cool,' said Isabelle, touching Shane's hand. 'Pile some more charcoal on the fire, Giles,' she added. 'He feels cold.' She glanced up at the small heavily barred window set high up in the wall. 'That damp, cold air from the river is coming in through there.'

Giles piled the wood into the fire basket, banging it down cheerfully with the iron poker and setting sparks flying around the small dungeon. Shane held out his hands to the fire and smiled. The warmth was comforting, almost like being back home again.

'Perhaps we should let him sleep,' said Isabelle with a worried glance over her shoulder. Shane noticed that the huge key was in Giles's hand.

'No,' he said, struggling to sit up. 'No, I'm not raving. Tell me about your brother. Why does your stepfather think that he is dead? When we arrived, I heard the captain tell him that your brother is alive. What about your mother? What does she say?'

'She died three years ago,' said Isabelle softly. 'My mother was French. Most of her relations live in France or in Wales and my father's relations are all dead. No, we have no one but our stepfather – until Hugh comes of age and can claim his estates, we are dependent on Sir John.'

'And he is a swine,' said Giles roughly. 'I was praying that he would be killed in a battle, but when it came to a fight he was too much of a coward to go, and he sent Hugh instead.'

'Has your stepfather sent a messenger to Drumshee?' asked Shane.

Giles shook his head. 'No messenger has gone. I asked the captain but he just shook his head and said nothing. I knew that he was angry, though, because his lips were pursed up and his eyes looked full of fury.'

'Then we must send a message,' said Shane eagerly. He looked at the beautiful Isabelle. Her eyes were full of tears and he felt that he could tear down the castle walls in order to bring back her brother to her.

'Could you help me to escape?' he asked eagerly. 'If I could escape I could make my way back to Drumshee – once I got across the River Shannon to Thomond I would be able to find someone to lend me a horse. I would ride back with your brother Hugh and see him safely as far as the Shannon.'

'Could you do that!' exclaimed Giles. 'Perhaps if I keep the key then we could smuggle you out at dead of night.'

'How could he get over the walls?' asked Isabelle.

'Perhaps I could steal the key to the front gate as well,' said Giles hopefully, but even he did not sound too convinced.

'And what about the portcullis? They lower that every night,' said Isabelle. 'And then there is the drawbridge – how could you lower that? Don't be silly, Giles.'

Giles looked a little crestfallen. Shane could see that he knew she was right though. In his mind he could picture the portcullis – that heavily barred gate that would hold out against anything other than a battering ram. Isabelle stretched out her hand and stroked her brother's blond head.

'Never mind,' she said bravely. 'We'll think of a plan, but before we do anything, this young knight will have to get strong and well again.'

'Call me Shane,' said Shane.

The beautiful girl blushed again, but she said softly: 'Shane must get well.'

'Probably you will get ransomed, anyway,' said Giles. 'My stepfather won't dare let Hugh stay in captivity, no matter how much he wants to. Too many people know that Hugh is still alive. He will exchange you for him.'

And so they stayed talking for hours. It seemed to Shane as if he had known Giles and Isabelle for the whole of his life and it seemed to Isabelle as if she had never seen anyone as beautiful as this young Irishman who stared at her with such devotion.

And then suddenly the door from above was thrown open, the light from the courtyard spilled down the steps.

'What's going on?' shouted a harsh voice. There was a heavy clump, clump, as a fat man made his way down the steps. He stood at the bottom staring at the frightened faces.

'Giles, how dare you steal that key? snarled Sir John de Courcy. You will have a whipping for this! And as for you, Madame Isabelle, get to your chamber and don't leave it again for this day.'

# Chapter 9

The morning that Father Simon left Drumshee with the letter for Limerick was a great morning. Suddenly, after all those weeks of rain, the sun had returned to Ireland. The soaked fields steamed and began to dry in the hot windy weather. The tightly closed buds of May blossom in the hedgerows burst open and showed their petals of clotted cream around a tiny crimson centre.

'Could I take Hugh for a ride?' asked Fidelma of her father.

'Surely, surely,' said O'Malachy. The weight of sorrow seemed to have lifted from his shoulders once the priest had set off with two men from Drumshee to escort him.

'I'll be in Limerick before the day is finished,' Father Simon had promised. 'First thing tomorrow morning I'll go to King John's castle. Perhaps your son will be with you before the next day is out, O'Malachy.'

So now all was joyful. Maur O'Malachy was flying around the castle ordering Shane's favourite spiced beef to be prepared for the next evening, making sure that his room was polished and the linen changed as if he had been missing for months rather than for days. O'Malachy himself had superintended the release of the cattle into the fields and had watched happily as they ran about like calves and plunged their noses into the soft green grass.

'Let Hugh take Shane's stallion, Fidelma' he said jovially. 'That's a ride that he won't get too often. Don't let him knock his legs, though. Shane is very particular about Bel.'

'I'll take care of him,' said Hugh gratefully when Fidelma translated. 'He is a beautiful horse. I owe my life to your brother, Shane, and I won't spoil his horse. If Shane had not saved me I would have been killed and I would never have come back here to Drumshee,' he paused for a moment and then said, very quietly, almost to himself, 'and I would never have seen you.'

He was a quiet boy, thought Fidelma, peeping at him under her lashes. He had a sweet, grave smile, but there was something slightly sad about his face, which roused her motherly instincts.

'You're lucky,' he said to her as they trotted side by side down the avenue. 'Your father and mother are so kind.'

'Tell me about your family,' she said shyly.

'I have only my sister, Isabelle, and my brother, Giles,' he said. 'Both my father and my mother are dead. My mother married again before she died. Her husband, my stepfather, is Sir John de Courcy. My mother was French so we were all brought up speaking French although we speak English, also.'

'Shane and I speak French,' said Fidelma. 'We learnt it from a French monk at Kilshanny.' She hesitated and then added: 'My father doesn't like the Normans coming here from England so he didn't want us to learn English or French, but when the priest from Kilshanny came and stayed with us for six months, my mother felt we should learn French — and perhaps some English.'

They rode on side by side until they came to a lake beside Mullaghmore Mountain.

'We should find gentians, here,' said Fidelma. 'Have you ever seen a gentian, Hugh? It's a tiny blue flower. It's so tiny that it is only the size of my smallest fingernail, but I have never seen anything so blue. Let's stop here, we can tie our horses to this hazel bush.'

Quickly she slid from the saddle and hooked Brideen's bridle over a stiff branch of hazel. Hugh swung himself off the back of the stallion and tied him carefully to the trunk of the tree. He held out his hand to her.

'Take my hand,' he said gently. 'I would not like you to slip and fall here. The ground is rough for you.'

His hand was warm and firm and Fidelma held it happily. She was quite at home on the broken limestone pavements – she and Shane had wandered around here many times in the year. She would not slip like many girls might do, but it was lovely to be looked after so carefully.

'Oh, look,' she said. 'There is a gentian!'

She bent down and picked the tiny flower. She smiled shyly. 'I'm going to make a wish,' she said. Ever since I was about four years old, I have made a wish when I found the first gentian of the year.'

She pressed the tiny flower against her lips and then closed her eyes. She made her wish:

Let Shane come back to Drumshee and Hugh stay here forever and ever.

And then she felt something else press her lips, not the gentian – that was soft, but cold and lifeless. Two warm, living lips pressed into hers. She opened her eyes quickly – hazel eyes looked into brown eyes and then they both closed their eyes again. But the kiss went on for a long time.

★ ★ ★

Two glorious days passed – two days of rides by the river, along the lanes, and across the moor. Hugh and Fidelma took Shane's hawk out to exercise him two or three times each day.

'Wave the lure when you get to the bottom of the hill and then I'll release him,' said Hugh and Fidelma galloped to the bottom of the hill, down beside the River Fergus and then waved the lure. Time after time, they did this, and each time the hawk flew straight as an arrow and landed on Fidelma's gloved wrist.

'It's almost as if Angus knows that Shane is not here and he has decided that I am second-best,' said Fidelma, 'but he'll forget about me as soon as Shane comes back,' she added happily.

But then the rain returned.

And that night the messengers from Limerick returned.

They were all seated in the solar, the fire cosily burning, its light flickering gold in and out of the shadows on the walls, when the sound of horsemen came through the open window.

'Shane!' whispered Fidelma. In a moment, she was out of the door and down the stairs, her mother, father and Hugh following her. Fidelma threw open the oak door, but there were only two men in the courtyard — two men leading a third horse and the third horse was riderless. Cian and old Brian had returned, but Shane had not.

'Did you deliver the letter?' asked O'Malachy.

'The priest went himself, O'Malachy,' said Cian. 'He went to the castle and he spoke to the constable, Sir John de Courcy. He told him that you held his stepson and that you were willing to ransom Shane by returning Hugh de Barry to him.'

'And?' O'Malachy's tension made the word snap out like an arrow from a tightly strung bow.

Cian shook his head. He was speechless. He looked at his companion for help, but old Brian averted his gaze. There were tears in the eyes of the elderly man who had taught Shane to ride his first pony.

Cian took a deep breath and then, in a rush of words, the terrible news came out: 'Sir John said that Shane would be hanged in a few days' time. As for the young Hugh de Barry, his stepson, he said that you were welcome to keep him and to string him up if that was any satisfaction to you. There will be no ransoming. Those were his very words.'

O'Malachy stared at Cian, speechless. Suddenly he was an old man. His weather-beaten face turned grey and he seemed to shrink and almost collapse into himself.

'O'Malachy,' said Brian. 'O'Malachy, the priest is staying in Limerick. He is going to get the head of the Augustine order to intervene on Shane's behalf. The priest said to tell you to trust in God.'

'What is it? What has happened?' Hugh turned urgently to Fidelma.

'Your stepfather will not ransom you,' said Fidelma briefly. The tears began to pour down her cheeks.

Hugh stood stricken, saying nothing, looking from one face to another.

'Trust in God,' yelled O'Malachy. 'Why should I trust in God? Why did God allow my only son to be taken from me like this? What can I do? I can't march on Limerick. It would take thousands of men to sack a castle like that.' He leaned against the wall, put his two hands to his head and groaned aloud. He looked like a bull at bay as he stared at his weeping daughter and then at his wife who had come walking slowly and stiffly out of the doorway into the courtyard, her face the colour of marble.

'What are you waiting for?' he screamed at the men who had come from kitchen and stables and fields and now stood around in a silent circle. 'Go on, do what his stepfather suggested, string up that boy. If the constable is going to hang Shane then we can hang this Norman knight here at Drumshee.'

Maur O'Malachy took a deep breath and walked forward. She put her hand on her husband's arm.

'Donal, we will not do this,' she said. 'No dishonour must be done in the name of our beautiful boy. Shane will be saved with the help of God and we must not do a deed like this. It's not this boy's fault. He has been abandoned by his stepfather.'

'You madden me,' screamed O'Malachy. 'Don't talk to me about God! Throw that Norman in the cellar, Cian. We'll hang him tomorrow unless word comes from Limerick. Diarmuid, you ride to the abbey in Limerick. Take the spare horse back with you. Bring us news, or bring us back Shane. Tell Father Simon he can promise anything – any money – anything as long as I can get Shane back again.'

Cian grabbed Hugh by the arm and dragged him roughly away. Diarmuid went towards the stables and then O'Malachy followed him. 'Take the black stallion with you. Shane . . .' he choked slightly and then recovered his voice, 'Shane will want to ride him if he is released.' Pushing the man aside he went into the stables himself. Fidelma and her mother followed and then stood back. O'Malachy had his arm around the black stallion and almost seemed to be holding on to the memory of his son as he buried his face in the animal's muscular neck.

'Where's the saddle, Fidelma?' he asked in a

muffled voice.

Fidelma fetched the flat leather saddle and without speaking helped her father to tie it on. She wanted to plead for Hugh's life, but she dare not speak in case she increased the savagery of her father's wrath. In silence, she watched as Díarmuid mounted on his horse and took the bridle of the black stallion in his hand.

'Why don't you ride over to O'Dea,' said Maur to her husband as he stood biting his lips and watching the man ride slowly down the avenue. 'He may have advice to give, may have contacts in Limerick. His overlord is Murrough O'Brien. The O'Briens have relations and friends everywhere. He may help us.'

O'Malachy stared at her with dawning hope in his eyes. 'I'll do that,' he said. 'Brian, saddle my horse for me. I'll stay the night,' he added, looking back at his wife.

'Do that,' she said.

'And if any news comes?'

'We'll send a messenger for you straightaway,' she finished.

Mother and daughter stood together while O'Malachy rode down the avenue.

'Come up to the solar,' said Maur gently. 'You're shaking. Stop crying now. Prayer is what is needed, not tears.'

Fidelma did her best, but she could not control herself. Her sorrow for Shane was deep and intense, but it was made worse by her feelings for Hugh. She could not bear the thought that the grave, brown-eyed, blond boy should have his life ended, should be killed by her own father. Wordlessly she shook her head. She didn't want to go indoors and shut the door. She wanted to stay outside, looking down the avenue, hoping against any possible hope that Shane might appear and Hugh might be released and that there would be a happy ending for them all.

'Are you thinking about Hugh?' asked her mother gently. Fidelma nodded. Another time she would have kept her feelings to herself; she would have been embarrassed that her mother had noticed, but now nothing mattered.

'I love him,' she wept, and then hated herself for mentioning such a thing when Shane was in such terrible danger.

'I know,' said her mother comfortingly. 'It will all work out, just wait and see. Let's go over to the statue of St Brigid and say a prayer to her that she will untangle the whole situation and send this Norman boy back to his family and bring Shane back home to Drumshee.'

Men and women thronged the courtyard, talking in low voices. They all stood back while their mistress and her daughter passed. Every eye followed them as they went out of the gate and turned left to go towards the little shrine of St Brigid under the big ash tree outside the outer wall.

The statue of St Brigid showed her as an old woman wrapped in a cloak. The face was old, and yet was young, and the quartz within the stone made the statue sparkle in the raindrops. Fidelma and her mother knelt down and buried their faces in their hands.

'St Brigid, keep them both safe, and let them both return to their own homes,' was Maur's prayer, but Fidelma prayed that both Shane and Hugh might stay forever at Drumshee. Somehow the prayer eased her mind and made her able to think, able to plan. Her father had talked of going to Limerick, and of the impossibility of getting in to the castle without thousands of men at his back, but there was one person here at Drumshee who would know how to get into the castle – King John's castle – one person who might be able to help. She had to talk to Hugh.

For the rest of the evening, Fidelma and her mother stitched on the wall-hanging that they were making for the Great Hall. It showed a young man, dressed like Shane, riding a black stallion, with his hawk on his wrist. The grass beneath his feet was embroidered with a hundred wild orchids and the sky was full of small birds flying away from the menace of the hawk.

Boring work, Fidelma always thought, but tonight she stitched with patience – though the time seemed endless. Eventually her mother yawned.

'I'll go to my chamber now, Fidelma,' she said. 'You go too and God bless you and keep you on this sorrowful night. Try to sleep. Tomorrow may bring good news.'

Fidelma obediently went to her chamber. She did not undress, or make herself ready for bed, though. She stood by the door until she heard the metallic click as the latch on her mother's door dropped into place. Then she took off her shoes, held them in her hand while very quietly she lifted the latch of her own door, eased it open, and then closed it noiselessly behind her.

 # Chapter 10

The kitchen was full of servants when Fidelma came in. Ann, the cook, was stirring a pot over the fire, Tom was stacking turfs of peat beside it, Brian was drinking some warmed ale, Donogh was sharpening his knife, and the two young maid servants were making pastries at the kitchen table. They all turned when she opened the door.

'Donogh,' she said. 'I want to go to the library to read. I can't sleep. Will you get me the key, please.'

He rose to his feet immediately. A look of sympathy passed from servant to servant. They had all heard the terrible news. None of them knew what to say. They just stood and looked awkwardly at each other. Donogh fumbled through the massive iron keys on the ring. In his embarrassment and haste he missed the key to the library.

'Just give me the ring, Donogh,' said Fidelma stretching out her hand. 'I know the library key. I'll put the ring back on the nail if you have all gone to bed when I have finished reading.' She looked from face to face and each set of eyes avoided hers. 'I think that I shall probably read until the early hours of the morning,' she finished gently.

Donogh was embarrassed. She had counted on that. They were all embarrassed. They would want her to be gone quickly. He handed her the bunch of keys and she smiled at him and walked out leaving the door of the kitchen open behind her and purposely making her footsteps sound loud and clear as she walked up the staircase towards the library. They must have no suspicions of her, now. She would have to wait in the library until the whole household was in bed.

Fidelma was a great reader and could always lose her troubles in a book, but tonight for the first time she could not read. She stood at the library window watching the moon. As she watched, she worked out her plan step-by-step. By the time that she had gone through all the details, the moon had moved from Drumevin hill right around until it stood high in the sky over the Isle of Maain and the bogland beyond. Two or three hours must have passed, she thought. Surely everyone was in bed by now. She had heard Ann and the maids go up to their bedrooms under the battlements of the castle at least an hour ago. Quickly she seized a small scrap-piece of parchment and wrote a note to her mother.

'*I have gone for a ride,*' she wrote. '*Don't worry. I will be very careful.*'

Cautiously she crept out of the open door of the library. She did not bother to lock it. Her mother's chamber was too near; she, also, would be getting very little sleep this night as she thought about her beloved son. Fidelma could not risk the click of the lock rousing her. She took the stairs, one step at a time, her soft slippers making no sound. In her hand she held the key of the cellar. She had found it by the light of the candle when she was in the library. It was the biggest and heaviest key of them all.

It was very dark as Fidelma found the door at the top of the stairs to the cellar. For a moment she regretted that she had not brought her candle with her, but she had feared to carry too much in case she dropped something. Carefully, with her left hand, she felt all over the door until her fingers found the hole of the lock. Slowly and cautiously she fitted the key into the lock. The lock was stiff and for a moment she worried in case that she had the wrong key, but then she put her two hands around its massive handle and managed to turn it. There was one loud click – it made her heart stop for a moment, but there was no sound from the sleeping household. Fidelma lifted the latch and pulled the door open.

Moonlight was streaming in through the little window in the cellar. She closed the door and was down the steps in a few seconds. The young Norman was lying fast asleep on the bare hard flagstones. She envied his courage. How could he sleep when he was in such terrible danger? She must wake him, but she must not allow him to call out in surprise. How could she do it? She smiled to herself, remembering that moment when they had found the first gentian of May. She knelt down on the floor beside him and pressed her lips to his.

He woke immediately; she knew that because immediately she felt his lips respond to hers. She took her mouth away and whispered in French: 'Hugh, speak in whispers.'

He took her hand in his, then sat up and gathered her into his arms. 'Don't sit on that wet floor,' he said. And then: 'You are so beautiful by moonlight, even more beautiful than by sunlight.'

'Hugh,' she whispered back. 'Hugh, you must escape. My father may do something terrible to you. You must escape now. I'll get you one of the horses from the stables.'

'And you?' he asked. 'Will I ever see you again?'

'I am coming with you,' she said firmly. 'Hugh, could we go to the castle in Limerick, to King John's castle? Could we rescue Shane? That is . . . that is if . . .' she paused. She read a question in his eyes. Was

Shane still alive? But somehow this night she was full of courage so she continued bravely. 'I know we can rescue him and I know that he is still alive.'

Hugh laughed gently and kissed her again. 'You stay here safely,' he said. 'I'll borrow your horse and ride to Limerick. I'll try to get your brother back.'

'No,' said Fidelma. 'You can't do that. You won't know your way. You can't speak Gaelic. My father will easily find you. I must come with you. If a man and a woman are riding together no one will suspect you. And we won't go the travellers' route to Limerick. I know what we'll do. We'll ride through the forest, through Kylemore. I know a secret way to Limerick, the way through the forest. My mother was fostered near Limerick at a place called Thomondgate – just across the River Shannon from King John's castle. Her foster-father is a merchant. He trades with the constable and his men at the castle. I have often ridden there with my mother. If we need anything, they will help us.'

'But your parents?'

'They will be happy when Shane is back,' said Fidelma firmly. She took his hand in hers and led him back up the stairs. Carefully she locked the door and took the keys with her. She would open the big gates in the courtyard and then hide the bunch of keys in the stable. The household would waste a certain amount of time looking for the keys before they could be sure that the prisoner had fled.

The moonlight still served them well. The stables were lit up as well as they would be on a winter's day. Without speaking Fidelma led out the horse that Shane used before he was given the black stallion. Hugh would be able to ride him. Then she got the two saddles and while Hugh was saddling his horse, she saddled Brideen. Brideen was easy to saddle and always stood very still so Fidelma was ready before Hugh. She looked around the stables. Shane's hawk, Angus, was still hunched like a ball of tight misery at the back of the stable.

'Hugh,' whispered Fidelma. 'Let's take the hawk. If we meet anyone in the forest they will not wonder what we are doing then.' In her mind Fidelma pictured Angus flying towards the battle scene at Dysart O'Dea. Perhaps, she thought, there will be some way to get in touch with Shane by using the hawk. Quickly she pulled on the leather gauntlet and tied the jesses around the hawk's leg to her own wrist. When Mother hears that the hawk is gone too, she is more likely to believe the note, thought Fidelma. In a few minutes they were both leading the horses out into the courtyard and then through the gates, and down the avenue. Once they reached the gate at the bottom of the avenue, they both mounted and set off towards Kylemore.

The forest of Kylemore was a place where charcoal makers dwelt. It had once been a great forest but in recent centuries the trees had been cut down to make charcoal and now the forest had many open paths and patches of hazel scrub At the top of one hill Fidelma could see the dull glow from a clamp – the heap of mud and twigs which allowed the wood to burn slowly and turn into sticks of charcoal.

'Let's turn down this way,' she said in a low voice to Hugh. 'The charcoal burners may see us. They are strange private men – mostly they have little to do with the other people who live around here, but they may tell my father that they have seen me. The name of O'Malachy is greatly loved around here. My great-grandfather found a treasure in Kilfenora and he helped many people around his birthplace.'

'So you are very rich?' enquired Hugh seriously.

'No,' sighed Fidelma. 'We used to be, but not any more. There has been famine in the land and we are now quite poor. My mother says we might have to leave Drumshee. Now we could do with finding another treasure.'

'That's good,' said Hugh calmly. 'I would wish you

to marry me and if you were too rich your father might not like you marrying a poor young knight. I think by the time that I am eighteen, my stepfather will have spent most of my money.'

'Is there no one to speak for you?' asked Fidelma indignantly.

'My mother's elder brother, Sir Nicholas Carew, lives in Wales. If I could get a message to him, he might come over and look into my affairs. My mother married my stepfather against my uncle's will and the families have had no contact since then.'

'My mother's foster-brother trades in skins and in Irish fur-lined cloaks. I know that he and his brothers trade with the people of Wales and the people of Bristol. Perhaps they might be able to bring a message to your uncle in Wales.'

'Perhaps,' said Hugh. He turned and looked down at her. With the moonlight shining on his blond hair he looked like a young god to her. Never in the whole of her life had she felt such happiness as she felt that moonlit night riding through the forest. They would rescue Shane; suddenly she was quite certain of that. They would send a message to Hugh's uncle. She and Hugh would get married and live in his castle in Cork. They would have many children and she would live happily for ever after.

Chapter 11

'I have never seen a man as beautiful as he is,' said Isabelle to herself. She sat by the window of her bedroom in the Constable's Tower in King John's castle, dressed in her shift and her nightgown, and prepared for bed. Slowly and dreamily she stroked the hairbrush down her long hair. One hundred strokes a night, that's what her old nurse had always said that her hair needed. Isabelle was happy to do it tonight. 'Rich gold' the beautiful young Irish man had said about her hair.

Isabelle had known many young knights at the castle. Young men from all the best Norman families around Limerick and Cork had served there and many of them had openly admired her. They were all fine young men; she had watched them riding in the courtyard, practising knightly arts of jousting with long spears and fencing with buttons on the tips of their swords, but she had never seen anyone as beautiful as Shane O'Malachy with his almost translucent white skin, his dark hair, and his eyes as blue as the sapphire jewels that her mother had worn when she was alive.

And just one hour ago she had heard the news: the Irish man would be hanged on Friday.

What can I do? she thought frantically. There was no point in appealing to her stepfather; she knew him to be evil and cruel. Whenever she thought of him she shivered. He had never done anything to her – though he had beaten both of her brothers savagely on the slightest excuse – but she shook with fear whenever she saw him. All three of them, even Hugh, went in great fear of him.

At that moment there was a knock on her door and her maid, Maud, came in:

'Lady Isabelle,' she said urgently, 'Sir John desires your presence in the Great Hall. He says to make sure that you are dressed in all your finery. Let me dress your hair.'

Quickly Maud brushed out Isabelle's golden hair, braided it and looped it. Then she took the white linen babette from the carved wooden chest and bound it around Isabelle's head so that only her face could be seen.

Now, the filet,' she said placing the gold filet across Isabelle's forehead and then placing the veil over the top of her head.

'I hate that babette,' said Isabelle crossly. 'I hate

having my head covered.'

'It's the latest fashion,' said Maud seriously. 'Now the green kirtle,' she added pulling out the gown from the chest and holding it out. Carefully Isabelle stepped into it.

'Now the surcoat.'

The surcoat was blue and sleeveless and it went on top of the kirtle. Maud wound an embroidered girdle with a hanging fringe of gold tassels around Isabelle's slender waist. Then she stood back.

'How do I look?' asked Isabelle with a smile.

'Very fashionable,' said Maud seriously. 'As fashionable as the Queen of England.'

Isabelle laughed. 'What do you know about the Queen of England?' she asked. 'I don't suppose you even know her name.'

'Yes, I do,' said Maud indignantly. 'Her name is Isabelle, the same as your own and as for not knowing anything about her . . .well, we may both see her before too long a time.'

Isabelle paled. 'What do you mean?' she asked. She glanced down at all her finery and suddenly understood.

'Tell me,' she said quietly. 'Tell me who is to be here tonight.'

'Young Sir Piers St Leger,' whispered Maud. 'King

Edward, Edward II of England, knighted him six months ago in London. He sent him to Ireland to fight Edward Bruce and Robert the Bruce. Now that Edward Bruce is dead, and Robert the Bruce has returned to Scotland, Sir Piers is going back to London.' Maud paused and looked at Isabelle proudly. 'And he wants to take a wife with him.'

'A wife? London?' repeated Isabelle stupidly. Suddenly she felt as if she could not breathe. Her life had never been pleasant here in King John's castle in Limerick since her mother had died, but the thought of leaving it now made her shake with fear. She felt she could not bear to leave her brothers, Hugh and Giles, and then she thought of the Irish prisoner, Shane, deep in the dungeon below the tower.

'Maud,' she said suddenly. 'What's the news about the young Irish prisoner? Does he know that he is condemned to death?'

Maud shook her head. There was a warning look in her eye.

'Forget about him, my lady,' she whispered. 'If Sir John knew that you had even inquired about him, he would be terribly angry. Just think about Sir Piers St Leger. Sir John wishes you to look well for him.'

So I'm to be paraded in front of this man like a mare to be sold at the market,' said Isabelle bitterly.

'He is a handsome young man, my lady,' said Maud. 'You are lucky. Other girls have been married off to men three times their own age. Women have to do what their fathers and husbands tell them to do. You have no choice. Come now. Sir John will be getting impatient.'

Sir Piers St Leger was a handsome young man. He was very dark, not too tall, but trim and active-looking with white teeth that flashed in a quick smile. I might have liked him if I had not seen Shane, thought Isabelle. For a moment she thought how easy it would be to say 'yes'. After all no one could blame her. How could she get Shane out of prison? There was nothing she could do – nothing except to try to forget, or at least, to pretend to forget. Steadily she walked down the length of the Great Hall, which was on the first floor of the Constable's Tower, and curtseyed to her stepfather and the handsome young man.

Giles was there, she was glad to see. He looked a little pale but was his usual merry self. Out of the corner of her eye, while her stepfather was making the introductions, she could see him scuttling around with the other pages, laying the silver dishes on the white linen that covered the table. This was going to be a great feast. The parents of the young Piers St

Leger were there and so were the Roche family from Fermoy and the Fitzgeralds from Askeaton. The St Leger family were staying with the Fitzgeralds at the moment, Maud had told her.

Any other time Isabelle would have enjoyed the occasion, the music, the compliments from Sir Geoffrey St Leger, but now all she could think of was the young Irishman, lying in the cellar below this tower – the beautiful young Shane who was condemned to death. She sat where she was told to sit, beside Piers St Leger, and waited impatiently until Giles approached her, knelt down, and offered to serve her from the dish of roast swan that he was carrying.

'Giles,' she whispered, keeping her voice down under the chatter of voices around her and pretending to fumble with her knife. 'Giles, Shane is condemned to die in two days' time – it will be on Friday when Sir John comes back from Askeaton. Can you get the news to him?'

Giles stared at her appalled. 'What good will that do to him?' he whispered. 'What can he do?'

Carefully Isabelle ladled some of the roast swan on to her plate and then held out her goblet to Giles' friend, Thomas, so that he could fill it with wine. She smiled at young Piers St Leger as he lifted his glass to her in a salute. She sipped the wine and then bent down again towards Giles.

'Is there any way that you can get a message to Shane?' she hissed. He shook his face. He looked panic-stricken and very young. She knew that she herself had to do the thinking. Suddenly an idea came to her and she smiled at him.

'Don't worry,' she whispered. 'I know a way to let him know. He is very brave and very determined. Once he knows the truth that there will be no ransom, he might manage to escape. No one, except Sir John, will wish him harm.'

'Giles,' boomed the voice of Sir John from the top of the table. 'Don't just serve your sister, boy. Attend to our other guests.'

Quickly Giles carried the roast swan to the other guests and then went back to get the roast peacock. This was to be a great feast, thought Isabelle; Sir John was sparing no expense to feed his visitors.

The dinner seemed endless to Isabelle. A thousand ideas swirled through her mind. The main dishes had been cleared away and the sweet course, a 'sublety' made from spun sugar in the shape of a boat on the Shannon, was carried in by Giles and Thomas and placed before Isabelle. As hostess, she had the task of carving it into small pieces, which were placed on plates and carried to all the important guests.

Yes, thought Isabelle as she sat back and daintily dipped her sticky fingers into a finger bowl brought to her by Giles, I know what I'll do. In her mind she pictured the small securely barred window high up on the wall of the dungeon. It was on the side of the river. There could be no escape from that window – even a three-year-old child would not be able to get through that – but a voice could get through it. If only she could shout down to him, he might just manage to overpower one of the guards and rush out. She couldn't shout down of course, but – and here was the wonderful idea – she could sing and warn him with the words of her song. Perhaps her stepfather would ask her to sing after dinner. No, she thought, I must make sure. He may not ask me and then the evening will be wasted. Resolutely she turned to the attentive young man beside her.

'Do you sing?' she asked shyly peeping under her dark gold eyelashes at young St Leger.

He shook his head, 'No,' he said and then added as she had hoped, 'but I would love to hear you sing.'

She lowered her eyelashes to hide the look of triumph in her eyes. That had worked easily, she thought.

'When will you sing for me,' persisted the young man.

'What are you two whispering about?' asked Sir John his broad red face split in a smile of triumph.

'I am trying to persuade Madame Isabelle to sing for me,' said Piers St Leger.

'After dinner, boy, after dinner,' said Sir John.

It's a long time since I heard him in such good humour, thought Isabelle. This marriage must be very important to him. I suppose the St Legers are very rich. Indeed, she thought, it's quite possible that Sir John has spent all of my marriage portion and if he manages to marry me off to the St Legers' son he hopes there will be no talk about it and no demands made of him. Quickly she swallowed a glass of mead. The honey in the drink would loosen the cords in her throat better than any wine. Tonight her voice would have to carry. She glanced over towards the window on the side of the river. The wooden shutters were drawn across it and were latched securely. Nevertheless, she would be able to demand that they be opened. In her mind she went over the words of the song that she planned on singing. It would just need a few words to be changed.

'You have the most beautiful smile of any lady I have ever met,' said Piers St Leger, leaning over close to her and looking longingly into her eyes. She was on fire with impatience for the dinner to finish but she forced herself to smile at him and to hold his eyes with hers. She must keep him amused and interested.

'I'm trying to think what song to sing to you,' she murmured.

'Sing me a song of love,' he whispered moving even closer.

'I'll sing you a song in French,' she replied looking at him keenly. Did he know French, she wondered. Probably, but it didn't really matter that much as people generally didn't listen to the words of a song.

He made a slight face. 'Sing to me in English,' he implored. 'I'm not good at French. The noblemen are beginning to forget French. Even at the court, now, King Edward sometimes speaks English.'

Isabelle smiled at him. 'English is the language of business,' she said teasingly. 'French is the language of love.' That's good, she thought with satisfaction. He would probably be the only one listening intently to the song. Her stepfather and the other guests would probably go on talking in low voices once the first few words were sung.

'Clear the board,' shouted Sir John. 'Bring in the harp. Now, Madame Isabelle, let's hear you sing.'

Giles and another page immediately carried in the harp and placed it in front of her and then they began to carry the dishes from the table back out to the kitchen. The long linen table covers were brushed free of crumbs and then folded up. Still Isabelle sat calmly there with the harp in front of her. It was only when everything was ready and every eye turned towards her that she began to give a few slight coughs and cleared her throat a few times.

'I must have air,' she declared. 'I can't sing here. Bring the harp over to the window.'

Without waiting for a word from Sir John de Courcy, Piers St Leger picked up the harp himself and carried it over to the window on the far side of the Great Hall. Isabelle smiled at him thankfully as she seated herself in front of it.

'Could you open the shutters,' she murmured innocently. 'The air is so hot and the smell from the candles gets into my throat.'

In a moment he had thrown open the windows and the cool air rushed in. From far below, Isabelle could hear the plop of a duck landing in the waters of the Shannon. She smiled to herself; the window of the dungeon was nearer than the river. If she could hear the duck, then Shane could definitely hear her voice singing. He knew French; he spoke it fluently. Now all that she had to do was sing the words of the old French love-song as clearly as she could. High and sweet, her voice rose up and drowned the chatter from the Great Hall and floated down through the open grating of the prisoner's cell at the bottom of the Constable's Tower.

'Fly, young man,' the French words floated out of the window. Below in the River Shannon a fisherman rowing a boat paused and rested on his oars. In the light of the setting sun on this May evening she could see his face turned towards the castle window. He was listening to the song. That meant that Shane could definitely hear the words. She smiled to herself in triumph and her high sweet voice rose even higher. 'Fly, my love,' she sang. 'Save yourself! On Friday morn your death will come, so fly now because I love you more than I have ever loved anyone before.'

# Chapter 12

Down in the dungeon of the Constable's Tower, Shane was idly stirring the fire with the poker that Giles had left behind. So far, he had been well treated – obviously the captain of the guards was expecting him to be ransomed any day. It made sense that Shane, the heir to The O'Malachy, should be exchanged for Hugh de Barry, stepson to the constable, Sir John de Courcy. Shane had been well-housed, well-fed, his wound had been treated, and was healing fast; in fact the only thing he had to complain of was boredom. He had enjoyed the visits from Giles and from Giles' beautiful sister, Isabelle, but these had abruptly ceased. Now he had no news, and he was beginning to get anxious. He hoped that Giles might be able to steal the key again, but it was unlikely. Sir John de Courcy would have probably given orders that the key was to be kept in a safe place now.

It was at that very moment that a sound came through the iron grating of the little window. At first Shane didn't know what it was – a sort of bang, he thought. Then he realised that the shutters of a window above his in this northwest tower had been thrown open. The cheerful sound of voices floated down to him. Then there was silence. Then a few notes from a harp.

And then a high clear voice began to sing. He had never heard the owner sing before, but instantly he knew that it must be Isabelle. For a few minutes he just took pleasure in the sound but then he realised that certain words were repeated over and over again. His French was good and he immediately made sense of the words.

'Fly, young man,' the sweet voice sang. 'On Friday morn . . .'

So he would be hanged on Friday! This was Wednesday evening; Shane had been keeping a close count of the days. That meant that he had only one day to escape. There was now no chance of ransom, no exchange of prisoners. Thoughtfully he picked up the poker and weighed it in his hand. It was heavy and strong. Yes, he could overpower his jailor when his next meal was brought. But what good could that do? Even if he reached the top of the steps the inner bailey would be full of men. There was no way that he could get through the bailey with just a poker in his hand.

And even if I did manage that, thought Shane, the heavy wooden doors would be locked shut, the portcullis outside the door would be lowered and the bridge across the moat pulled up.

Then suddenly he heard another sound coming through the little grated window high in the wall. It wasn't singing this time; it was the sound of oars dipping into the river water. Of course, thought Shane. The River Shannon is just outside the wall of this cell. If only that window were bigger I could get out and dive into the river and swim across to Thomondgate.

Over near to the door there was a rough table. It was made from an immensely thick chunk of wood and was as solid as a stone table. It had been used for hammering out the coins when this dungeon had been the king's mint for silver coins almost two hundred years ago. Shane grasped the rough wood of the leg in his left hand and dragged the table cautiously across the floor until it was under the window. Then he flexed his right arm. It was wonderfully improved. It hurt him to move it, but he could move it and that was all that mattered now. He would have to use it if he was going to swim across the river.

Then Shane looked all around the little room.

The fire was low and it gave little light. The candle, however, burned brightly. He decided to extinguish it before he started work. If the room was dark and someone opened the door quickly it would give him a moment to get down from the table and to pretend to sleep. No one guarded him too closely. They knew that he was expected to be ransomed so he was treated more like a hostage than a prisoner.

Carefully he climbed up on to the table. Now he could reach the little window. The stones on the left-hand side of the window were small and the lime plaster was old and damp. Using the poker he was able to lever one of the stones until it was loose. Leaving it in place he dug away at a second one. This one was easily loosened also. Shane felt a rush of excitement. At this rate he would soon be able to take out the iron grating and make a hole large enough for him to wriggle through.

The night was black outside by the time Shane had loosened all of the stones. He could work more quickly now. Everyone in the Great Hall had retired to bed and only the tramp of the guard's boots on the ramparts and an occasional laugh from the night watch soldiers in the inner bailey broke the silence. The work was astonishingly easy, thought Shane. He couldn't see, but he could feel that he had loosened at least ten stones. Carefully he shook the iron grid across the window and it came away in his hand. Taking a chance he lowered the grid on to the table and piled the loose stones beside it. Now he could get on with widening the gap.

The gap was large enough for him to stick his head right through, and also one of his shoulders, when Shane came up against an obstacle. Instead of loose stone there seemed to be something different, something that rang like a bell when he tapped it with the poker. He passed his fingers over it. Yes, it was certainly made of iron. Why would there be a sheet of iron there in the wall behind all those small square stones?

Leaving the puzzle of the solid piece of iron aside Shane tried the poker on the stones on the right-hand side of the little window. Nothing yielded. He explored with the tips of his fingers but all he could feel was smooth hard stone with no little crevices. It must be just one large stone, he said to himself.

Then he tried the top of the little window and it was the same thing. A huge solid stone spanned a distance of over twice the width of the window. It was the same at the bottom of the window. The poker was now getting blunt and with his fingers Shane could feel that the tip of it was slightly bent.

His wounded right arm was throbbing – it was healing well, but the flesh was still raw and tender – and he felt deeply tired.

I'll wait until the light comes up, he thought. It's the middle of May. Dawn should come at about four or five – too early for many people to be awake. I'll work better when I can see what I'm doing and I could do with a few hours' rest. Carefully he replaced the grid of the window and the small stones as well as he could. Then he threw some more wood on the fire and lay down on the bed with his face turned towards the window. The light would wake him as soon as dawn came.

Shane felt much better – stronger and more hopeful – when the first grey light of dawn came through the little window. He swallowed some ale from the jug that the guard had left the evening before and took a few quick bites from a hunk of bread while he was climbing on to the table. He would have to work quickly. Already there was a smell of smoke and the scent of newly baked bread on the wind. That meant that the bakers were already at work making small loaves of bread for breakfast.

One glance at the huge stones around the three sides of the little window made Shane frown with annoyance. Each one of them would take half a day to dislodge and even when he got one out; there would probably be another one just as big behind it. These walls must be as thick as two men lying head to toe. The window was his only chance. Again he took out all the small stones on the left-hand side. Now he could see the iron sheet plainly. It wasn't a sheet, he realised a minute later. It had rounded corners: it was some sort of iron box. The box was double the size of the window; if he got it out he would have just enough room to escape that night.

Shane always looked on the bright side of things. In an instant his courage came flooding back and his cheeks flushed with excitement. His blue eyes sparkled as he dug around the soft wet mortar that held the box in place. Once he had loosened this box and removed it he was sure that he would be able to escape out through the space. The box was very near to the back of the wall. There would probably just be some stones on the outside. He could easily dig these out, slip out the grating of the little window, dive into the River Shannon and swim across to Thomondgate.

The hunting dogs in the kennels of the bailey were now beginning to bark and yelp with excitement. This meant that the kennel servants were bringing the dogs their breakfast of brom bread –

bread soaked in broth made from boiling bones and scraps of meat. After that, the men-at-arms would be fed, and then his breakfast would be brought to him. He had less than half an hour before he needed to restore the wall and drag the table back to its usual place.

Still Shane did not panic. He worked on steadily and methodically, gently scraping all around the box and dropping the loose pieces of plaster through the windows down into the Shannon. Very quickly the box moved under his hand. He took it out; it was very heavy; so heavy that he almost dropped it. He was about to place it on the table when he realised that there was something in the box, something that clinked and shifted within it. He raised the lid and stared inside. For a moment he could hardly believe it, but then his red lips curved in a smile that stretched from one ear to the other.

Inside the box were hundreds of silver coins. They had the head of King John stamped upon them. He had often seen coins like this – but never so many. The box must hold at least five hundred coins.

I'm rich, he whispered, and he had to stop himself from shouting the words aloud.

In a flash he understood what had happened. He remembered what the captain had said: 'This used to be the mint – they used to mint coins here in the time of King John. They would melt the silver here, pour it into moulds, turn them out onto this stone slab and then stamp the king's head on them on this old table over here.'

So perhaps someone had decided to rob the mint, perhaps someone who had worked at the mint. The thief might have hidden the coins in the iron box and then covered it over with stones and, for whatever reason, had never come back for his treasure.

Now if only I can get out of here I will take this with me and I will be able to restore the fortunes of Drumshee, thought Shane, and then, just at that instant, he heard a shout coming from the parapet on top of the wall near the tower where he was kept as a prisoner.

'Henry,' shouted the voice. 'Take a loaf of bread and a jug of ale to the prisoner. I'm busy with the repair of the portcullis.'

What am I going to do? thought Shane. I haven't time to fit the box back into the wall and to replace all the stones carefully, and to drag the table back.

Two minutes later the bolts of the heavy door were drawn back and a young soldier stood at the doorway at the top of the steps with a jug in one hand and a hot loaf in the other.

By now most of the soldiers at the castle had met Shane. In the beginning he was considered as a short-stay guest; it was assumed that he would be exchanged for young Hugh de Barry. Shane's ready smile and friendly manner had made him popular with all who brought his meals to him. Even when it was whispered that no ransom was to be accepted, no one would have considered him to be anyway dangerous. So the young soldier got a shock when his way was barred by an aggressive young man with a poker in his hand who was shouting at the top of his voice: 'Take that food out of here. I don't want it. Get me the constable. The first man who comes in here without the constable will have his brains knocked out.'

The soldier backed away hastily, dropping the loaf on the ground and spilling half of the ale from the jug. In a moment he had slammed and locked the door.

In one leap, Shane cleared the whole flight of stairs. There was no way that the soldier could have seen anything was amiss with the wall while he was on the top of the stairs but now the wall had to rebuilt before more soldiers came back. As hastily as he could, Shane placed the heavy iron box in the wall, stacked the small stones neatly one on top of the other, balancing each one of them as carefully as he could making sure that the white-washed edges were to the outside. It looked good enough; no one was likely to test it.

Then suddenly, just before he could jump down, a bird flew against the window. Its yellow eyes glared at him through the bars. It was Angus; Shane had no doubt about it. He could see the small scar on the forehead where Angus had been clawed by a falcon when he was young. If Angus was there, his father must be somewhere near. Everything was going to work out! Shane jumped from the table, a rush of happiness bubbling and sparkling inside of him. He dragged the table back to its usual place and lay down on the straw bed gazing at the fire.

When the captain of the guards came in, with ten men carrying drawn swords to his back, he found the prisoner smiling placidly at him, the poker concealed inside the straw of his bed.

'What's the trouble?' he asked.

'I just wanted to see the constable and find out when I am to be exchanged?' said Shane innocently.

'Oh, is that all,' said the captain glaring at young Henry who was hovering nervously in the background. 'Well, why didn't you say so without making a fuss? Anyway,' he finished sounding rather awkward and embarrassed, 'you can't see the constable today. He's away all day. He won't be back until tomorrow.'

 # Chapter 13

The sky had changed from inky blackness to that grey light that comes just before dawn when Hugh and Fidelma reached Thomondgate outside the city of Limerick. They reined in their horses on the western bank of the Shannon and stood gazing across at the tall grey bulk of King John's castle with its six tall limestone towers and the crenellated walls joining them. The castle was quiet at the moment. Just one light showed and that was from a small window low down in the north-western tower.

'That's the dungeon,' said Hugh pointing across the river.

Fidelma sucked in a breath. 'Is Shane there?' she asked.

Hugh nodded. 'Probably,' he said.

Fidelma strained her eyes. She had wonderful eyes. Almost, she fancied, she could see the head of Shane at that small barred window. On a sudden impulse she untied the jesses which bound the hawk to her wrist and released Angus.

Straight as an arrow the bird flew across the River

113

Shannon. She could barely see him now, just a pinpoint of darkness, but he had definitely gone straight to that barred window low down on the Constable's Tower. For a moment he lingered there and then he flew back across the river and landed on her wrist.

'Shane is there,' said Fidelma with confidence in her voice. 'He is there and he has seen Angus. He knows that we have come to rescue him.'

Hugh turned to look at her. There was a smile on her lips but her face was very pale and there were dark circles around her hazel-coloured eyes.

'You need to rest,' he said gently. 'We have ridden all night. Let me take you now to your mother's foster family and we can hear the news there.'

Maur's foster-mother, Laoise, was at the door when they rode up. Her face lit up, and then clouded over, when she saw Fidelma's face. 'It's true then,' she said, and there was a catch in her voice. 'That lovely lad, Shane, is a prisoner at the castle. We heard the news yesterday. Jonathon brought some wine to the castle and someone told him. But come in, come in . . . you look worn out.'

Hugh jumped from his horse and threw the bridle over the post by the gate He untied the hawk from Fidelma's wrist and tied its jesses to the post by the door. Then he held out in his arms for Fidelma. She fell heavily into them. Suddenly she was worn out. He held her close for a moment and then carried her into the house. Laoise tied Brideen to the post and then followed them.

'Put her there,' she said. 'Put her on the settle by the fire. Lie down, my pretty,'

Fidelma lay stretched out on the seat. Every muscle and bone of her body ached with exhaustion. Laoise fussed over her, covering her with a fur rug and holding a hot, spiced drink to her mouth. She did not ask about Hugh; all her attention was on Fidelma but when Jonathon, her husband, came into the room, he stiffened with amazement.

'You're young de Barry, aren't you?' he asked, speaking French. Without waiting for an answer he turned to his wife. 'That's Sir Hugh de Barry, Sir John de Courcy's stepson,' he explained.

Laoise stared at him with astonishment. 'What's happened?' she asked in bewilderment, turning to Fidelma. 'How did you meet him? Have you been to the castle?'

'He's been a prisoner at Drumshee,' said Fidelma. She was so tired after being awake all night that her lips felt stiff and her eyes ached. Hugh gave one swift look at her and then appealed to Laoise.

'Is there anywhere that Fidelma can rest and sleep for an hour or so and then I'll explain my plan to you. I thought of it as soon as I heard that your husband is a trader with a merchant boat of his own.'

Fidelma's tired eyes opened wide at that. Hugh had said nothing of this while they rode through the forest of Kylemore. So he had been planning all the time!

'Come into my chamber, Fidelma,' said Laoise. 'It's at the back of the house and nothing will disturb you there. I'll draw over the shutters.'

'But what about Shane?' asked Fidelma trying to force herself to shed her tiredness.

'Leave Shane to me,' said Hugh with a confident smile.

Suddenly she relaxed. She gave a tremendous yawn. She could leave it all to him and rest for an hour or so, she thought. She pulled herself to her feet and stumbled to the door with Laoise's arm around her.

As soon as they had gone out, Hugh turned to Jonathon. 'You have a boat on the River Shannon, do you not?' he asked.

'I do,' said Jonathon.

'You know my stepfather, Sir John de Courcy?'

'I do,' said Jonathon again.

'And you know the manner of man he is?'

'I do,' said Jonathon for a third time.

'Then you won't be surprised,' said Hugh, 'if I tell you that he refused to ransom me and sent a message to Drumshee saying that they should hang me. In return he will hang Shane, Fidelma's brother.'

Jonathon nodded.

'I want to rescue Shane before my stepfather hangs him,' continued Hugh. 'We're not too late, are we?' he added quickly.

Jonathon looked at him. Hugh saw the questioning look in his eyes.

'You can trust me,' he said rapidly. After a minute's silence Jonathon nodded.

'I'll trust you,' he said.

'We're not too late?' asked Hugh again.

Jonathon shook his head. 'You're not too late. I hear the execution is planned for tomorrow morning.' He thought for a moment and added: 'your stepfather is away today. He left the castle late last night – the man who takes the night-soil from the privies told me that. Sir John will not return until tomorrow morning. They will not hang young Shane before he returns.'

Hugh jumped to his feet. Suddenly everything seemed possible.

'That's luck that I dared not hope for,' he said rapidly. 'I've been thinking and thinking about how I could get into the castle unseen, but now there is no problem. I shall just ride across the bridge and tell the guardsman at the gate to the castle that I have escaped. Sir John will have given no orders about me. He will rely on the Irish hanging me.'

'And when you get into the castle . . .?'

Hugh hesitated for a moment but then spoke out boldly.

'I plan to steal the key and let Shane out of the dungeon,' he said.

Jonathon smiled. 'Not an easy thing to do,' he said.

'I'll manage,' said Hugh confidently. 'I know all the soldiers and the palace servants. The young knights and squires and pages are all my friends.'

'And what then? You can go and come as you please; you are the constable's stepson. No one will dare challenge you. But how can you get Shane out? I know what it's like at the front gate to the castle. They are preparing for a raid by O'Brien of Thomond. The two gatehouses are full of men. When I went in there today I saw an arrow aimed at me from every loophole in the towers. And what am I? Just a merchant with a cartload of wine! And I was no stranger to any of them!'

Hugh smiled – a secret, knowing smile. 'Once I get Shane out of that dungeon I know what to do. Forgive me if I do not tell you more. It's not that I don't trust you, but it is safer for you to know nothing.'

Jonathon shrugged his shoulders. 'The young have a great belief in themselves,' he said. He looked at Hugh for a moment and then smiled. 'And it often carries them through a business that no man of my age would dare attempt,' he added lightly.

'Yes, but I need your help, too,' said Hugh, and now a note of doubt crept into his voice. Was this too much to ask of a man who had never met him before, of a man who might lose everything if the plan was discovered?

'I see,' said Jonathon. He looked into the brown eyes of the young man and liked what he saw. He gave a little nod as if he had decided something in his mind.

'Tell me what you want done, and, by God's mercy, if I can do it; I will,' he said solemnly.

 # Chapter 14

Fidelma was still fast asleep when Hugh left the merchant's house at Thomondgate. He took Shane's hawk from the stable, tied the jesses to his wrist, then mounted the stallion and trotted slowly down the street and towards the bridge across the Shannon. This was the test. If he were stopped at the bridge, he would know that his stepfather had issued orders. He approached the men in the guardhouse slowly, with every nerve pricked and alert. He would still be able to turn around and go back if there was any hesitation on their part.

However, nothing but astonishment and pleasure showed on the faces of the men guarding the bridge.

'We heard you had been captured,' said one of them, coming out of the gatehouse, his face lit up with delight.

'I escaped,' said Hugh. To his surprise, he had no difficulty in making his voice sound happy and excited. He saw the man look curiously at the hawk on his wrist. He smiled. The more often he explained, the more true the explanation would sound. 'I stole this hawk and took him along with me to make it look as if I were just out hunting,' he said lightly and was relieved to see the man nod with understanding.

Hugh took a deep breath. This was working out well 'I want a bath and a good meal now,' he added. 'I've been riding all night.'

'You won't find Sir John at the castle,' replied the man, 'but your sister and young Giles will be pleased to see you. Maud, the lady-in-waiting to your sister, was saying that the Madame Isabelle was heart-broken about you. We all heard that you were not to be . . .' he stopped abruptly as the captain came out from the gatehouse behind him giving a warning cough.

So everyone knew that I was not to be ransomed, thought Hugh as, with a friendly wave, he walked his horse across the bridge. Still, he consoled himself; no orders have been given to stop me or to arrest me. Why should Sir John do that and risk news coming to other Norman Lords of what he had done? Why not let the Irish do his dirty work for him, allow them to hang his stepson and then he himself could draw the revenues from the de Barry estates until Giles was old enough. Suddenly he stopped, his eyes widening in dismay. What would happen to Giles?

Would Giles be in danger then if Hugh were gone? He would have to take Giles and Isabelle with him when he left King John's Castle forever today. Today was the only day that he could do that. He cast a quick glance at the western wall. Yes, his plan would work; he was sure of that.

A cart piled high with sacks of flour was waiting outside the castle gate. The drawbridge was already open and the portcullis, that immense piece of stout oak sheathed in iron to protect it from fire, was being slowly raised by two men using a winch to wind it up.

'Sir Hugh,' one of them shouted down and then turned towards someone else in the background. 'Sir Hugh is back! He's alive and well.'

Hugh waved and smiled and waited with the cart until the portcullis was completely raised and the gates swung open. Once the way was clear, he courteously waited for the miller to bring his cart in first. It would never do to rush, to look unsure at this point. Gently he stroked the head of the hawk with his gloved finger and glanced around him. In the entrance passage, right under the murder holes, where boiling oil could be poured down on attackers, he could see the captain of the guards waiting. This would be his greatest test. If Sir John had taken this man into his confidence then he might just take Hugh prisoner until the constable returned. All were busy at the gate tower, he noticed. They were expecting an attack. From the Armourer's Room he could hear a hammer beating out a sheet of iron. That would be for leg armour and breastplates, he guessed. The old chain mail did not provide enough protection from the iron tipped arrows which could inflict a deadly wound. The fletchers were busy making arrows, also. The barrels beside them were rapidly being filled with the oak shafts each one trimmed with a goose feather.

'Hugh,' it was the captain of the guards. There was no smile of welcome on his face and his eyes had a wary, shuttered look. Hugh placed his hand carelessly on his sword and cast a quick glance behind him to see whether the way was clear back across the bridge. The captain of the guard drew near and put his hand on the horse's bridle His head was close to Hugh's and he spoke in a low tone.

'It's not so healthy around here for you now, Hugh,' he said and his voice was heavy with meaning. 'Is there any relative that you could go and stay with for a while? I advise going now and not waiting until Sir John comes back tomorrow morning.'

Hugh hesitated. It was tempting to confide in this man, tempting to try to get his brother and his sister out of the castle as quickly as possible, but then he remembered Fidelma. He had to rescue her brother. Honour, as well as love, made it impossible to give up on doing that now. He gave the captain a careless smile.

'Oh, I'll be all right as soon as I have a bath and a meal,' he said lightly. 'I never catch any diseases: I'm as healthy as a wild duck,' he added, deliberately misunderstanding the man.

The captain stepped back. He would say no more; he had already said too much for wisdom. If Sir John ever heard of what he had said, he would suffer for it. Hugh nodded at him, smiling boldly, and moved along the entrance passage and out into the bailey. The captain had not remarked upon the hawk; possibly the man was too preoccupied, too worried.

The bailey inside King John's castle was a large six-sided space with four large drum towers at the north western, south western, north eastern and south eastern corners and two gate towers on either side of the gate facing north. There were high stone walls joining the towers and lining these 'curtain' walls were the thatched wooden bailey buildings: the craft shops for blacksmith, carpenter, candle maker, slaughter house, meat store, grain store and kennels for the hunting dogs. On the south side of the bailey was the Great Hall with the chapel beside it. These two buildings were made from stone, but the other buildings were all made from wood and they had thatched roofs well below the curtain wall.

The space in the middle of the bailey was full of people: some young squires were practising at the quintain trying to duck the heavy bag of flour as it swung around, the pages were playing camp ball, some men-at-arms were cleaning rust spots from armour by rubbing it with oiled sand, carpenters were hammering, trying to repair the trebuchet which was used to shoot stones over the wall at the attackers, other men-at-arms were chipping stones to the right size to be used in the trebuchet. The noise was so great that when Giles ran up to Hugh they were able to speak together with no fear of being overheard.

'Hugh!' said Giles, 'I . . .'

'Listen,' interrupted Hugh in a tense whisper. 'We're all in great danger from Sir John. Help me now, Giles. You go on playing camp ball with the other pages while I go up to Isabelle. As soon as you see the captain of the guards go to have his dinner, then come up and let me know immediately. Go now. He is watching us. He knows a little of Sir John's mind, I think, and he is not easy.'

Giles gave a quick nod, started to run away, but then turned back.

'Where did you get the hawk?' he asked curiously.

'Stole it,' replied Hugh blandly. Giles raised his eyebrows, but then ran back to his game landing an exuberant kick on to the ball and scoring a goal for his team. A great cheer rose up; Hugh smiled to himself. He guessed that Giles was relieved to have his older brother back and to have the responsibility taken off his shoulders. Rapidly Hugh crossed the bailey, waving to the women who were baking the dinnertime loaves in the kitchen and quickly went through the door of the mews where the hunting birds were kept.

There was no one inside the mews so Hugh tied Angus to the perch nearest the door – he would want to get him out quickly and silently that night if all went well. He put some food and water before the hawk and then went out again, crossed the bailey and entered the northeastern tower.

Isabelle was sitting on the window seat of the solar, thoughtfully stitching at a tapestry of a hunting scene for the wall of the Great Hall. She did not look up as he came in. Hugh glanced around the room keenly. Even though four tall candles of finest beeswax burned in the huge fathom-high candlesticks yet the room was dark and full of shadows. Hugh had no desire to be overheard by Isabelle's lady-in-waiting, Maud. She was not to be trusted; he was sure of that. He crossed the room and sat on the wooden chest beside her, placing his finger on her lips for a moment.

'Hugh!' she said and flung herself into his arms.

'You are alone?' asked Hugh.

'Yes,' she replied steadily. She did not question him. She must guess that something was amiss; Hugh knew that instantly.

'Isabelle,' he said in a hushed tone. 'I must get you out of here. Sir John wants me dead and you and Giles are in danger also.'

She showed no surprise. 'Sir John wants me to marry Sir Piers St Leger,' she said evenly.

Hugh hesitated, taken by surprise. 'In that case,' he said, 'you may be safe. Piers St Leger is a worthy man. He and I were knighted at the same time. I remember us kneeling side by side in the chapel on the night before we were knighted. I liked him. Perhaps if you marry him you will be safe.'

Isabelle shook her head. 'No,' she said. Her face flushed suddenly. 'Hugh,' she said, 'I love someone else. I love Shane O'Malachy. I know I hardly know him, but I love him. Please believe me. Don't try to make me marry Sir Piers. He is nothing to me.'

Hugh laughed. 'Let me tell you a secret,' he said. 'I love Shane O'Malachy's sister. Her name is Fidelma. Now listen carefully while I tell you my plan.'

Hugh had just finished telling Isabelle the plan when there was a pounding of young feet on the spiral staircase outside, the latch of the iron-studded door was lifted and Giles burst in.

'Hugh,' he said breathlessly. 'The captain of the guards has gone for his dinner.'

'Good!' said Hugh springing to his feet. 'You go back down, go to the dining hall. Isabelle, you go with him. Say that I am in the garderobe washing and that I want a good meal. Make a bit of a fuss. Ask for lots of things. Make sure you keep an eye on the captain. If you see him rise, then engage him in conversation.'

'He won't,' said Giles confidently. 'He is a great eater and when Sir John is away he always takes a long time over his dinner.'

Hugh waited until he could see them cross the bailey and then stole down the spiral staircase. He stood in the shadow of the door for a moment. Yes! He was in luck. A man emerged from the door of the kitchen carrying a rough wooden tray. As he came nearer Hugh could see that it was Henry, the youngest of the guards. He relaxed happily against the door. Henry was not too bright; he would believe anything that Hugh would tell him.

'Bringing the prisoner his dinner?' enquired Hugh in a casual tone as the man came near.

Henry jumped. 'Oh, yes, Sir Hugh,' he said.

'I'll go down with you,' said Hugh. He didn't expect Henry to argue with him but he was surprised when the boy's face lit up.

'Oh, would you, Sir Hugh,' he said. 'I'd be glad of that. You see this morning when I was bringing him his breakfast he threatened me. The captain wouldn't believe me; the prisoner was as quiet as a dove when the captain came down, but he did threaten me.'

'Well, I'll be to your back with my sword,' said Hugh thankfully. He cast a quick glance across the bailey. No, there was no sign of the captain emerging from the hall. Quickly he seized a candle from the bracket inside the doorway. 'Give me the keys,' he said a note of brisk authority in his voice. As he expected, Henry handed them over meekly. Hugh took them in his left hand. The key to the dungeon was the largest one. Hugh studied it carefully by the light of the candle. He would know it again, he decided. It had an extra long piece at the top and it was quite unlike the other keys.

'I'll open the door for you,' he said aloud. He noticed with amusement that Henry remained in the shadows until Hugh had greeted the prisoner. Obviously he was still nervous of Shane.

Shane did not look like Fidelma; Hugh had expected that he would. Fidelma was brown-haired and hazel-eyed: this young man was white-skinned with blazing blue eyes and jet-black hair. His personality was different also: Fidelma was gentle, dreamy and shy. This boy's face was alive with a smile that went from ear to ear. He was quivering with life, and fun, and joy of living. Even here in this dark dungeon, in the depths of the castle, he shone with the burnished air of a young deer.

'I am Hugh de Barry,' said Hugh formally. He spoke French, and Shane instantly replied in the same language.

'I know it – I have seen you before. You were the one that snatched up the banner when de Clare was felled. I saw you cross the river.'

Hugh bowed. 'And I think you were the one who spared my life,' he said. With a quick glance at the guard, he added in rapid French, as low as he dared, 'And I hope to do the same for you.'

The guard's face did not change. He still stood there holding out the tray in front of him as if it were some sort of strange-shaped shield.

Shane took it with a smile. 'Thank you,' he said in hesitant English. 'I hope I did not frighten you this morning. I was upset.'

The young guard, Henry, looked relieved. His face softened into a sympathetic smile. He hid his embarrassment by shaking up the straw mattress and Hugh immediately saw an opportunity.

'Fetch another mattress,' he ordered. 'That straw is turning to dust. We must treat our prisoner well.'

Without a word, Henry raced back up the steps leaving the keys in Hugh's hand. Hugh waited until he heard the crash of the closing door and then turned to the prisoner.

'Shane,' he said. 'Your sister and I have a plan.'

Shane nodded and smiled. He did not seem surprised. Life had always been good to Shane and he expected that he would be rescued.

'I've tried to get through that little window,' he said eagerly. I nearly managed it but the stones on the outside are too big. I'd need a pickaxe, not a poker.'

Hugh glanced briefly at the little window. 'No,' he said. 'There is no need for that. I have another plan. I am going to release you once the castle is quiet. You will need to be ready.'

Chapter 15

To be ready was easy, thought Shane; to wait was unbearable. There was only one thing that he could do and that was to store all the silver coins safely so that when he escaped he had them with him. There's enough here to save Drumshee, he thought. He knew how desperate with worry his father had been during the past year. The terrible weather had brought famine to the land; the tenants, whose crops had been destroyed and whose livestock had died, could pay no rents. With this amount of silver, Drumshee could be safely brought through the crisis.

Quickly he pulled off the fine linen undershirt that he wore. The linen was strong and new, but eventually, with his sharp white teeth, he managed to rip one edge. Now he could tear a long strip. Carefully he placed half of the coins inside it and knotted them into a bundle. Then he tore another strip and knotted the rest of the coins into that piece of linen. Now he had two bags of coins. He took the embroidered *crios* or sash that his mother had made for him on his tenth birthday. She had woven a St Brigid's cross into the fabric of the *crios* and had told him that that he must always wear it so that St Brigid would protect him against all harm and danger. Quickly he breathed an earnest prayer to St Brigid that this night would see him safely back home again. Then he took the *crios* and knotted the tops of the two bags of coins with it and slung them around his waist, one on each hip. Then he put his tunic back on again and buckled his leather belt loosely. The coins would be safe there unless he was taken prisoner again. He clenched his teeth and set his jaw. He vowed he would not be taken prisoner and that he would go back to Drumshee and care for his father and mother and sister. And then he sat, and he waited.

It was hard to tell the time inside the dungeon. The small window on the west showed the streak of the setting sun, and then a pale light, and then no light at all. It would be a dark night; Shane felt a rush of optimism and thankfulness at the thought. There did not seem to be a moon – though it should have been full moon. The night must be cloudy, he thought – all the better for the business that this night would bring before dawn arrived.

Shane was almost dozing when he heard a faint scratching sound. And then the key was turned in the lock. Hugh brought no lantern or candle with him, but Shane knew him by sound of his footstep. He made no sound, just stood up and waited. Hugh came nearer so that the light of the fire fell upon him and then he beckoned soundlessly. Shane walked up to him and stood close.

'Throw that cloak over you,' whispered Hugh. 'It's a cloak belonging to my squire. He is black-haired like you and if you muffle the cloak around your face, you may get through the bailey unchallenged, if by chance you are seen.'

Rapidly Shane slung the cloak around him and pulled one fold across his mouth and nose. He asked no questions; the plan was Hugh's and he trusted him. With a springing step he followed Hugh and went without hesitation into the bailey.

Hugh stopped to lock the door to the dungeon while Shane stood well back in the shadows. No one was watching them. A couple of men lounged by the fire in the iron basket on the northeastern side of the bailey and from overhead, on the parapets of the walls and the towers came the metalled tramp of the watchmen's boots. Hugh made a quick signal with his hand and Shane moved further back into the shadows. Hugh was waiting for something; he could see that.

And then Giles emerged from out of a thatched

wooden building on the south side of the bailey. He did not look towards Hugh, but walked steadily across the bailey towards the western side. Hugh moved across and joined him, but the quick backward motion of his hand again warned Shane to stay where he was. There was a pause. None of the men throwing dice by the light of the fire took any notice of the two brothers, but then a door opened at the foot of the Constable's Tower and a slim figure shrouded in a cloak stepped quietly out. It was Isabelle. Her pale blond hair was covered with a hood that cast a deep shadow over her face. Nevertheless, it was obvious that she was immediately recognised. The rattling of the dice stopped and every head swivelled around. From above Shane could hear the booted feet of the watchman pause. For a moment there was complete silence. The men around the fire were staring with astonishment. Shane held his breath. It was obvious that Isabelle had never appeared in the bailey at midnight like this.

Without hesitating Isabelle walked swiftly down the bailey to where Hugh and Giles stood. She spoke to them in a low voice. Shane strained his ears but he could not hear what she said. He could hear Hugh's answer though. 'Go and get him, Giles,' he said.

For a moment Shane's heart stopped. He was

bewildered. Surely Hugh was not betraying his hiding place. However, Giles, with a nod, ran across the bailey and went into the mews and brought out the hawk. It's Angus, thought Shane and now he understood.

As soon as the men saw Isabelle bend over the hawk and stroke its head, the dice game started again with noisy shouts and cries of despair and the solid rhythmic beat of the booted feet on the parapet above was resumed. Shane's heartbeat slowed down and he leaned against the wall, alert, but relaxed. Hugh had obviously planned this carefully. He, Giles and Isabelle strolled across the bailey. 'We'll fly him through the sally port,' said Hugh in a voice that was meant to carry across the bailey.

Shane smiled to himself. The plan was a good one. The men might briefly wonder why they were flying the hawk at night – and through the sally port, which was the emergency exit door from the castle, placed low down in the wall next to the river, but after all, Hugh was the stepson of the constable of the castle and if he wished to fly his bird by night in the company of his brother and sister it was none of their affair.

There was a flaring torch stuck in the wall close to the door leading down to the sally port and Shane could see Hugh very clearly by its light. Quivering with anticipation he watched. Hugh gave one last careful look around and then a quick flip of the hand. Shane began to move along, keeping his back to the wall and his eyes fixed on the men by the fire basket.

Then he saw Hugh reach over and lift a torch from its metal bracket. He, Isabelle and Giles walked through the door carrying the torch. Now the door was in deep shadow, but Shane could see that they had left it open by a few inches. In a moment he had reached it and slid through, carefully and noiselessly shutting it behind him. He heard a key turn in the lock. There was a strong smell of pitch, but no light. Hugh had extinguished the torch. Then Shane felt a hand grope and seize his. He smiled to himself in the darkness. The hand was not Hugh's; this was a slim, soft hand and faintly, below the stench of the pitch, he caught the sweet smell of lavender. Quickly he raised the hand to his lips and kissed it.

The stairway to the sally port was steep and broken in places, but Hugh trod the steps without faltering and the others pressed closely behind him. Then Hugh rattled the bunch of keys and in a moment the wet west wind swept in through the opened door. Outside was the River Shannon.

Isabelle gave a soft gasp. 'The moon has come out,' she whispered. 'The clouds have blown away.'

'We can't afford to wait,' said Hugh through gritted teeth. 'We must act now. This is our last chance. Sir John will be back by morning.'

'I see the boat,' whispered Giles. 'Do you see, Shane? That's the trader's boat. He will come across for us once we give the signal.'

Shane strained his eyes. There were several boats on the river but he could immediately pick the right one out. He knew the boat well. He could see Jonathon, his mother's foster-father, on board. There were other men also, probably Jonathon's sons. But one figure was a girl in a hooded cloak. To his surprise she suddenly raised her arm and waved something in the air.

'It's Fidelma,' whispered Hugh. 'This is the signal we arranged. The boat will come for us once we send the hawk.'

The hawk on Hugh's wrist gave a soft muted sound. Shane knew that sound well. Angus had seen his lure. Quickly Hugh released the bird from his jesses. Straight as an arrow he shot across the river. The light from the moon was very bright now and Shane had no difficulty in seeing the bird alight on Fidelma's wrist.

Instantly the anchor was drawn up. The night was so still that they could hear the sound of it coming out of the water. With no word spoken, the sails were unfurled and as the north-east wind caught the sails, the boat swiftly crossed the river.

'They're making for the bridge,' whispered Giles.

'They'll be able to turn to the right at the last moment,' said Hugh in low voice, 'but in the meantime it will seem to the watch on the parapet that the boat is just delivering wine.'

At midnight? queried Shane in his mind, but he said nothing – only prayed that Hugh was right. Some of those men from the castle were not too clever. He was watching the boat intently. It was coming across the broad river very quickly, so quickly that he could now see Fidelma's face and he could see Angus perched on her wrist.

'She's turning,' whispered Giles, his voice thrilling with excitement.

The boat was now lying parallel to the castle walls. The sails had been lowered and a couple of hefty men with oars were sculling cautiously, and as noiselessly as they could, along under the wall. Soon the boat would be within their grasp.

And then, at the very moment when Jonathon had picked up a coil of rope ready to throw it – at that very moment, there was a loud banging and battering at the door behind them.

'Sir Hugh, Sir Hugh,' shouted a voice. 'Are you there? Sir Hugh, the prisoner has escaped.'

 # Chapter 16

'Oh, my God,' whispered Hugh. 'We have no hope now. They'll batter down that door in a few minutes. They'll have archers up on the parapets. We'll never get away.'

'Hugh, listen,' said Shane. 'Get on that boat immediately. Go on,' he insisted. 'You may all be killed if you don't do as I say. I have a plan.' Quickly he stretched out his hand with an impatient gesture, caught the rope and drew the boat in to the edge of the castle wall. 'Isabelle,' he said urgently, 'as you love me, get on that boat, you too, Giles, and you, Hugh, you must go with them. They'll need a man with a sword.'

Shane untied the belt full of the silver coins from his waist, placed it in Isabelle's hands, then took her in his arms and swung her on to the boat, Giles climbed in after her. Hugh swung one long leg in, and then hesitated.

'Come on, Shane,' he said. 'We have a chance. Let's keep together.'

Shane shook his head. 'No chance that way,' he

said briefly. 'We have a chance if you do as I say. Jonathon, take the boat downstream, keep close to the eastern side of the river until you are out of range of the arrows and then moor your boat on the far side of St Munchin's island. I will join you soon. You know how well I swim.'

With that Shane snatched the keys from Hugh's hand and in two minutes was back up the steps to the door that led to the sally port. Quickly he fitted the key to the lock, adjusted the squire's cloak so that its hood fell over his face, pulled open the door and then shouted out in French:

'The prisoner is in the south-western tower. Quick, all of you! Follow me! Sir Hugh has him covered from the side of the river. He cannot escape that way.'

The guardsmen fell back uncertainly as he pushed through them. Not giving them a moment to think, he took off at high speed running down the bailey and was in the door of the south-western tower before they had ceased stumbling over each other's toes.

'Follow me,' he shouted again, and he clattered up the spiral staircase. He had reached the door of the first chamber before they came into through the tower door. Quickly he closed the chamber door behind him, looked at the lock – not a big lock – which key was it? He looked keenly at the lock, looked back at the bunch of keys, selected a key, fitted it in . . . yes, it worked. The lock clicked.

'You villain!' he shouted in French and then he lowered his voice. 'You'll never take me alive,' he shouted in Irish. Quickly he grabbed a sword and a buckler shield from the wall. Steel clanged on steel! Then Shane lifted his voice in a scream of fury and then, next, a grunt of pain. Now he could hear the guards' feet pounding up the spiral staircase. He waited until they had reached the landing and then he clicked the key loudly in the lock. Now the door was locked again.

'Help,' he screamed in French. 'He has locked the door. Help! He will kill me. Break the door down,' he roared – in English this time – just in case the guardsmen did not speak French – but he was careful to speak English with a French accent.

And then for a good measure he beat out another few clashes of sword on shield, and gave another roar of pain and then a scream of triumph in Irish.

That did it! Now they knew that the Irishman would possibly be the victor. They had to do something now. He heard them run, clattering down the stairs. They would be going for some heavy rams to break the door down. They would have to go right down into the bailey again and drag the rams up the steep curving spiral staircase. Shane reckoned he would have a good five minutes before all was discovered. Now was the moment to escape. Cautiously and soundlessly, he placed the shield and the sword on the floor, slipped off the Norman squire's cloak, opened the window and without a moment's hesitation dived into the Shannon' waters that flowed beneath the window.

His pointed arms hit the water cleanly and the river parted to let him in. It was a good dive and he did not feel winded by it. He struck out immediately swimming to the west where he could see the island of St Munchin, downstream of the castle and its bridge. The water was not too cold on this May night and Shane was a strong swimmer. He struck out as silently as he could. There was no sound from overhead – obviously the guards on the parapet had run down to join the other men in hauling the ram up into the south western tower. That was a bit of luck – the waters of the Shannon were so smooth his black head might have been glimpsed as he cut his way along the river, strongly swimming downstream towards St Munchin's Island.

The tide must be ebbing, thought Shane. There

was very little effort needed to swim. The river seemed to bear him along. I'm past King's Island now, he thought exultantly, ignoring the ache from his wounded arm. The English colony and, of course, the castle, were all situated on King's Island; the River Abbey curved around the southern edge and it flowed into the Shannon making the great river run even faster. Now he was progressing twice as fast, churning through the fast-flowing water.

Hardly five minutes had passed by the time that he reached the island of St Munchin. There was no sign of Jonathon's boat, but Shane did not worry. Jonathon would have lowered his sails and hidden the boat on the northwestern side of the island. He could see a sandy beach on the eastern side of the island and he struck out towards that. After another minute he could touch sand beneath him with his toe. He glanced quickly over his shoulder. There was no sign of pursuit and no one at the castle could possibly see him from this distance. He stood up and waded for the shore, the water parting as his long legs strode through it.

The island was flat and sandy. It had the remains of an old abbey on it, but now nothing lived there but rabbits. The Normans had originally brought rabbits with them when they came to Limerick, to supply fresh meat. They had placed pairs of rabbits on various islands on the river and the rabbits had multiplied over the last hundred years. Everywhere that Shane looked he saw white tails scuttling away in front of him and diving into sandy burrows under the short green grass. He grinned. Suddenly he felt incredibly light-hearted. He had been rescued from the castle and the girl that he loved was just over the hill from him.

And then the great alarm bell at the castle began to toll, archers – so far away that they looked like tiny models – appeared on the castle parapets shooting arrows into the Shannon's waters, and, worst of all, Shane could see a Norman boat move off from the small stony beach near the bridge. The chase had begun!

Shane scaled the hill. When he reached the top he took a quick glance upstream towards the castle. The light boat was making very quick progress. The sooner we're off this island the better, he thought, and then started to run as fast as he could downhill. He could see Jonathon's boat moored in a cove below him. As soon as he appeared over the brow of the hill Jonathon shouted an order and the sails were raised. Isabelle was there at the side of the ship; Hugh, with his arm around Fidelma, was beside her, and Giles stood ready to throw the coiled rope over the side of the boat. In a moment Shane was splashing through the shallow water and then he had grabbed the rope and was pulling himself, hand over hand, up on to the boat. Instantly Jonathon hauled up the anchor and with an east wind behind them the boat moved swiftly downstream.

'They're behind us,' gasped Shane. 'They'll overtake us soon. They've got one of those light skiffs of theirs and it's moving fast.'

'Curses,' muttered Jonathon. 'I won't be able to turn off the Shannon now and slip up the Fergus to get you all safely back to Drumshee. With this north-easterly wind the sails won't help much – the wind would be almost in our faces if we turn off to go up the Fergus. We'll have to keep going. Their boat is lighter than ours, not a sea-going boat, but we should be able to keep ahead of them until we reach the sea. They won't dare to follow us then. Their boat would be smashed to pieces by the heavy waves out there in the Atlantic.' He stopped and looked at the five young faces before him. His mouth lifted in a grim smile. 'Well,' he said. 'Nothing for it! I had planned to go next week, but I'll have to go today. We're off to Wales.'

 # Chapter 17

All the way down the River Shannon, Jonathon's boat kept ahead of the soldiers' skiff. The wind could not have been better. The sails of the boat swelled with every ounce of wind and the boat leapt through the water as if it were alive and understood the danger. The smaller lighter skiff was behind and although the men were rowing like demons, they could not catch up with the sail-driven boat. If the wind slackened, however, they would be at the soldiers' mercy. Shane could see the archers poised on the deck, arrows fitted to bows, ready to fire as soon as they could shorten the distance between the boats.

'Go below, my darling,' he said to Isabelle. 'Go with her, Fidelma,' he added. 'You will just be a worry for us on deck. There is nothing that you can do, here.'

Fidelma lifted her chin. She said nothing, but instead she turned and started to look through the chest full of bows and arrows. Isabelle joined her, handing bows to her brother and to Shane and then a smaller bow to Giles. Fidelma sorted out the arrows, filling each quiver, and then handing them out. Shane smiled. He noticed that Fidelma had laid aside a bow and some arrows for herself. She was a good shot – there would be no possibility of sending her below now. She would insist on remaining. Isabelle also picked out a bow for herself and carefully tested its string.

'Go below, Fidelma and Isabelle,' urged Hugh, but the two girls took no notice of him, either.

'Trim the sails,' shouted Jonathon, and his sons sprang to do his bidding. The northeastern wind had veered. Shane licked a finger and held it up to the wind. He turned around, towards the pursuing boat, and felt the wind strong and cold on his face.

'We've a head wind,' he said joyfully. 'It's due east now. They'll never catch us if this keeps up.'

At that moment an arrow came speeding across the water. It fell short, but it was a magnificent shot. Jonathon cast an uneasy glance over his shoulder. But, by then, the sails had been turned to catch the every possible puff of wind, and the boat jumped forward. The distance between them and the skiff was increasing every minute. Suddenly an order was shouted. The skiff turned north.

Jonathon chuckled. 'They're trying to cut us off,' he said. 'They fancy we're going to turn into the

Fergus. Of course they know that Shane came from Thomond. Still, they must think we're fools. We could never outdistance them going upstream and against the wind on the Fergus.'

The channel where the River Fergus entered the Shannon was broad and fast flowing. The tide was ebbing so the new water flowing in was dragged out to the west towards the sea. Jonathon's boat sped along with the prow ploughing through the white foam, which frothed over both sides.

'We'll never be able to hold steady enough to aim at this rate,' said Shane in Irish, grabbing the rail and laughing across at his sister.

'I could,' she replied, and then turned to Isabelle and said something in French. The two girls laughed. Shane smiled at them. Happiness was sparkling inside of him. Every minute they were getting further and further from the soldiers' boat. He could see it slow down.

'They've given the order to turn,' said Hugh at his shoulder. 'Look, they've lifted the oars from the water, now see just the men on the starboard side are rowing, the boat is turning.'

'You're not worth the trouble of pursuing, Shane,' said Giles teasingly. 'You're just not important enough.'

'They'll get a shock when they go back and see

that we're gone,' said Isabelle.

'Not too much of a shock,' said Hugh. 'The captain of the guards was on that boat and I swear that his eyes met mine. He will not be surprised. He knew the three of us were in danger from Sir John. He more or less told me so.'

'Wait until old guzzle-guts gets back from Askeaton,' chuckled Giles.

'That's Askeaton over there,' said Jonathon pointing to the south bank of the river.

'What a shock he'd get if he could see us on our way to Wales,' gloated Giles, leaning over the side of the boat and feasting his eyes on the castle of Askeaton.

'What are we going to do, Hugh?' asked Isabelle.

'Could you land us in Pembroke, in Wales, Jonathon?' asked Hugh. 'Somewhere near Carew Castle, if that's possible. My uncle, Sir Nicholas Carew, owns Carew Castle.'

'I can take you to the very door,' said Jonathon. 'I have bought flour there many times. There is a tidal mill attached to the castle. It's a miracle that mill! I've never seen anything like it. The movement of the tides grinds the corn.'

'You will be very welcome at my uncle's house, Jonathon,' said Hugh with that grave courtesy that made Fidelma love him so much. 'My uncle will welcome all who have been kind to me, my sister and my brother – and all whom I love,' he added in low voice taking Fidelma's hand in his.'

'Will he get your estate in Cork out of Sir John's hands, Hugh?' asked Giles eagerly.

'Undoubtedly,' replied Hugh. 'I was at fault not to seek him out earlier, but I kept hoping for the sake of the memory of our mother, that Sir John would not be turn out to be as bad as I feared.'

'So Isabelle and I will be able to live with you, and not at the castle in Limerick,' pursued Giles.

'You will certainly be able to live with me,' said Hugh smiling, 'with Fidelma and myself,' he added. 'But as for Isabelle, I think she may have other plans.'

'She certainly has,' said Shane drawing Isabelle close to him. 'Isabelle and I will live at Drumshee. Now that I have these bags of silver we will have no money worries. Look Fidelma – show her, Isabelle – there is enough there to keep Drumshee safe.'

'So we'll all be married before June,' said Hugh happily.

Jonathon surveyed them uneasily, though there was a twinkle in his eyes. 'No more of this talk,' he said firmly. 'Wait until I get all five of you safely with Sir Nicholas at Carew Castle. He can talk sense to you.'

They laughed at him. Nothing could lower their

high spirits. Jonathon had a consignment of wine on board – meant for the castle, he said with a grin – and everyone had a glass with their supper of fresh trout landed from river and new bread baked the night before by Laoise. No one wanted to sleep; they were all too excited.

By the first light of morning they were at the coast of Kerry. They met a merchant ship coming in from the Atlantic. Jonathon lifted his voice and yelled across the water. The other ship turned and came towards them.

'Take a message to the wife for me, Brian,' shouted Jonathon in tone that was more like a fog horn than a human voice. 'Tell her that all is well and I am taking the trip to Wales now while the wind is with me. Tell her to be sure to let our friends know that all is well.'

The other seaman waved, his words lost in the wind, but they could see his head nodding.

'Shane and Fidelma could have gone back with him,' remarked Giles innocently.

'Oh, no!' said Shane and Hugh, their voices blending as one in their haste, while Fidelma and Isabelle blushed and smiled discretely at each other.

'No, that wouldn't be safe,' said Jonathon. 'They'll be watching all the ships coming in for the next few days. That's what they would expect us to do – go out to the mouth of the Shannon and then turn back. No, it's safer to take you all the way to Wales. Laoise will send a message to Drumshee. You'll be worrying about your parents, of course,' he added sternly.

'Of course,' chorused Shane and Fidelma hastily, but a minute later Shane had his arm around Isabelle and Fidelma had slipped her hand into Hugh's.

'You might as well come and take the tiller, Giles,' said Jonathon with a smile. 'I'll teach you to sail. No place here for the two of us at the moment.'

The wind was in the northeast until they rounded the southernmost tip of Ireland, where Kerry meets Cork and then it suddenly dropped. They had a few days of calm weather then the wind veered around to its usual south-western point.

'Well, God is on our side,' said Jonathon with satisfaction. 'If this keeps up we will be in Wales before the week is out.'

'Don't rush,' said Hugh hastily. 'We're fine. We're all enjoying the sailing.'

Jonathon grinned but rushed off to shout at one of his sons who was lowering a sail.

'Are you worrying about meeting Sir Nicholas?' asked Fidelma gently.

'I suppose so,' admitted Hugh. 'All I know of him is that he is my mother's brother. He has never shown any interest in us or sent any messages to us.'

'Wait until you meet him before judging him,' advised Shane. 'After all, Sir John might have received messages, but not passed them on. Don't worry about it anyway. I never worry about anything. I find that things usually turn out for the best. If I hadn't got captured at the battle of Dysart O'Dea then I would never have met Isabelle and you would never have met Fidelma. Let's enjoy the rest of the voyage.'

The time passed very quickly. By early evening on Sunday the boat reached the harbour of Pembroke and turned upriver towards Carew Castle.

'It's as big as King John's Castle at Limerick,' gasped Fidelma.

'I hope Uncle Nicholas is friendly,' murmured Isabelle, looking apprehensively at the huge grey castle with its towers and battlements.

'He will be,' said Shane confidently.

Shane was right. Sir Nicholas Carew was a huge fat man, as fat as Sir John de Courcy, but there was no other resemblance. He was warm-hearted and friendly and his wife was motherly. She took immediate charge of Isabelle and Fidelma bearing them off for hot baths and a change of clothing. Her own daughters were grown up and had married, but there were plenty of fine dresses left behind. Isabelle and Fidelma appeared at table that night looking splendid.

Sir Nicholas bought the consignment of Spanish wine from Jonathon and placed an order for some marten furs to be delivered in a month's time.

'You will be able to take Shane and Fidelma back with you then,' he said in his loud voice as Jonathon prepared to embark. 'Everything should be safe for them by then. Sir John will not hunt too long. I propose to see King Edward about Sir John's guardianship of my nephews and about the property in Cork. Sir John won't have much to say for himself by the time I've finished with him.'

One month! The four young people looked at each other. One more month together and then . . . Separation? It didn't seem bearable. Even Shane did not have much to say, for once.

'Have you talked with your uncle about you and Fidelma and about Isabelle and myself?' he asked Hugh.

Hugh nodded. 'He just laughed and said: "One thing at a time. Let's sort out the property and then we'll talk of marriage". He's going to London tomorrow to see King Edward.'

Shane said no more. This magnificent castle at

Carew with its many towers, its huge Great Hall hung with silks and satins, the table spread with costly silverware all worried him. Would Sir Nicholas think that he, Shane O'Malachy, was worthy of his niece?

★　★　★

When Sir Nicholas arrived back from London three weeks later he was in great humour. The packhorses behind himself and his squire were laden with presents. There were lengths of white satin and cloth-of-gold for a new gown for Isabelle, crimson silks and satins for Fidelma, a new sword for Shane and another one for Giles. For Hugh, however, he brought the best present of all.

'I've spoken with the king,' he said. 'He has agreed that you will take the management of the lands and castle of Barrymore into your hands from now on. There is good steward there and if it's found that any of the land has been sold by Sir John, then the king will force him to make recompense. I think you will find all in good order, though. Sir John is not a brave man. He might have taken the estate over if you and Giles were out of the way, but I don't think he would have dared to sell it when you were so near to coming-of-age.'

'And Fidelma?' asked Hugh hardly able to breathe

with excitement.

'The king has agreed in principle,' said Sir Nicholas. 'Now it will be a matter for her parents. But now I want to talk to you about Giles. I have no son – my daughters are well married and their sons will have lands to inherit. I would like Giles to inherit the castle and lands of Carew and perhaps, if he is happy to do so, to bear the name of Carew. What do you think?'

'I think he would be very happy,' said Hugh.

'Then I'll ask him,' said Sir Nicholas, and he left before Hugh could ask him anything further.

'But did he say anything about Isabelle and myself?' asked Shane while Sir Nicholas and Giles were off on a tour of the Carew lands.

'Nothing,' said Hugh. 'I did not have the opportunity to ask him, but I will the next time we are talking privately.'

But it seemed as if Sir Nicholas was avoiding them both. He gave no opportunity to either Hugh or Shane to talk to him. He spent a lot of time with Giles and the steward. And Isabelle and Fidelma seemed to be spending most of their time with Lady Carew and the sewing maids. Hugh and Shane were left on their own walking disconsolately around the shore.

'That's Jonathon's boat,' said Hugh, a few days

after Sir Nicholas's return from London.

'Good,' said Shane. 'Now I will have news of my father and mother.'

They both ran down to the shore. Jonathon and two of his sons disembarked and then ran up a plank against the side of the boat.

And then, from out of the small cabin, came O'Malachy followed by Maur.

'Shane!' they both said and that was all. Fidelma, followed by Isabelle came running down a few minutes later. Isabelle and Hugh stood back while the O'Malachy family were re-united once again.

'Father, Mother,' said Shane 'I want you to meet Isabelle. Here she is. I want to marry her.'

Maur looked at her beautiful son. She could have denied him nothing, but when she looked at the sweet-faced Norman girl with her corn-blond hair and her dark eyes, she held out her arms to her.

Fidelma drew in a deep sigh of relief. Now it was her turn and she hoped everything would work out. 'Father, Mother . . .' she began, but O'Malachy burst out laughing.

'We know all about it,' he chuckled. 'Jonathon brought a letter from Sir Nicholas. Why do you think we are here? We've come for the two weddings, of course?'

'And why do you think I brought back the fine new cloth from London?' demanded Sir Nicholas coming out to join them. 'We've just been waiting for your parents to arrive so that the weddings can take place. The priest has everything ready, the cooks have been making pies and pasties for the last week, and the girls' dresses are ready down to the last stitch. The weddings will be tomorrow.'

And so Hugh and Fidelma, Shane and Isabelle were married the next day.

Shane and Isabelle went back to Drumshee with O'Malachy and Maur. The silver that Shane had discovered in King John's Castle was enough to keep them living comfortably for the rest of their lives.

Fidelma went with Hugh to Cork, in the province of Munster, in the south of Ireland. They, and their children, and their children's children, lived there in that rich land of forests and fast-flowing rivers until two hundred years later, when the great wars between Garret Fitzgerald, Earl of Desmond, and Queen Elizabeth of England ended with the eviction of the people of Munster from their land of fertile soil to the barren wet cold lands of Connaught.

And then it was that the Barrys of Cork came back to the land of their great-great grandmother, Fidelma of Drumshee.

Author's Historical Note

The battle of Dysart O'Dea took place on 18th May 1314. Every time that I go from my home to Ennis, the market town of Clare, I pass the marshy ground where it was fought and I often wonder what would be found there if archaeologists excavated it. Would there be swords, arrows, a brooch that pinned a chieftain's cloak, a piece of silver from the time of Edward II, or perhaps the bones of the men and horses that died there?

The story of the battle is as I have related it in the book – the Normans, led by de Clare, were enticed on to the marshy land beyond the river by the sight of a small force of men driving a herd of cattle across the ford at that spot. No one knows who thought of that strategy – various clans have claimed it, but in my story I have given the credit to Shane O'Malachy from Drumshee. The Irish forces, who had lain hidden in the woods and bushes around the lake, emerged and fell upon the Normans once their horses were plunging and sticking in the heavy mud. Richard de Clare, six of his knights and many of his advance guard were killed instantly.

The people of County Clare are very proud of this battle as the Anglo-Normans were driven out of the kingdom of Thomond (Clare) on that day and did not return until the days of Elizabeth I, over two hundred years later.